To Mary ~~~~~~~~~~ Clark

For convincing me to write my story as a novel.

# The
# True
# Volition

## Hexalogy

Part One:

# Deviance

# The True Volition Hexalogy / Part One: Deviance / Table of Contents

Part I: Innocence (Purity)


Chapter One: Graduation                                    08-17
Chapter Two: House Party                                   18-33
Chapter Three: Fourty-Five Months, Twenty-Four Days
34-47
Chapter Four: The Bar                                      48-55
Chapter Five: A Long Time                                  56-73


Part II: Deviance (Aberrance)


Chapter Six: Initiation                                    75-85
Chapter Seven: Fever                                       86-95
Chapter Eight: Let's Fight                                 96-105
Chapter Nine: The Road                                     106-121


Part III: Revelance (Anagnorisis)


Chapter Ten: Hotel Lakeshore                               123-136
Chapter Eleven: The Big City                               137-146
Chapter Twelve: Genesis                                    147-159

\*\*

"I love you… so, much."

\*

Is your life a series of random events? Or is it a well-orchestrated plan, known only as destiny? Futurology is the science, art, and practice of postulating possible futures. Practitioners stress the importance of alternative, and plural futures, rather than one monolithic future. They frown upon the limitations of predictions and probabilities, versus the possible creation of endless preferable futures. Like many modern-day thinkers, futurologists consider David Kellogg Lewis's theory of modal realism to hold great weight. Modal realism is the view that all possible worlds are as real as this one.

Was I born for a reason? What is my purpose? Life, in all of its complexity, is what you make of it. The meaning of life is discovered by those willing enough to create it for themselves. Some do not have the strength. Others do not care to make any meaning. But for Nathan Farrantino, reason and purpose are not created by him. They are crafted by entities far greater than he could ever conceive. On the day of his high school graduation, these forces begin to turn the cog of 'destiny', changing Nathan's life... forever.

*

# PART I
## Innocence
### (Purity)

# Chapter One:
## ~Graduation~

The Milky Way hung in the late-night sky, with a tone accompanying a menacing violin crescendo. There were no clouds and the moon had hidden away, leaving the stars in all their majesty to shine down on Earth. Anyone looking up would have seen a true spectacle. The vastness of space had swallowed the sky, and in its deep silence something stirred. A thing that could not be seen, or heard, or touched; but it stirred, nonetheless. In the suburbs of a quiet Canadian neighbourhood, a young man named Nathan tossed and turned, asleep in his bed. Light was null. His brow was furrowed and nostrils were flared. Beneath his eyelids his pupils raced to and fro from each side of his skull.

"Beware the quarter of year," a faceless woman whispered out of the void of sleep, her voice sounding ancient beyond years. "For with it will bring fire and darkness; the likes of which your kind has never seen." Her melodic voice was trailing away, "Alone, you must stop it…" laid the last message for Nathan's unconscious mind to absorb before his senses melted.

Feelings, fleeted. Crisp, sharp darkness churned a shrewd complexity into infinity. Endless unseen fractal loops of something not yet observed overlaid omnipotence. Abstractions made distraction but began to pull into focus; shapes, things. Objects objecting realism. There was something. It was zooming; closing in. His skinny, pale arm was reaching for an object: an impossibly black orb. The orb displayed his features as a dark creature rose from below to overlay its face onto Nathan's. It sat only for a moment, but the face was notably demonic: twisted, three-eyed and grinning. The horror show flashed to an inactive laptop screen showcasing in its reflection his sleeping body, and then… darkness consumed him. In the depths of the void, sounds swirled around; voices. They were familiar to Nate, but he couldn't make out what they were saying. Then one word began to stick out. One word which he immediately recognized: 'Nathan.' Again and again, they called his name. Old friends and family members calling out to him from his memories. Winds began to build, giving Nathan's mind unease. Through the scramble of conversations that were happening all at once, his attention focused in on particular voices among the crop.

"Over here!" one boy yelled.

"You never want to see me succeed," Nathan heard himself say.

"I don't think you're ready," said a coarse, unfamiliar man. The voices continued, and under all the noise, Nathan began to hear screaming… Screaming coming from what sounded like thousands of people, all very far away.

"Just give it back!" his younger self pleaded. Rising anxiety spilled over at an overwhelming rate.

"I love you… so, much."

That voice was familiar, but the phrase was not. That was the voice of Vivian, a girl from Nathan's school. But she never said that to him before.

"What," his voice echoed, "am, I?" He didn't know why he said it, but the echo brought a silence to the void. And a deep, menacing voice answered back…

"Human."

Footsteps clicked and echoed in the dark. They echoed slowly and loudly through the blackness as they neared. Nathan was helpless and terrified; all he could do was listen. Closer and closer the footsteps came. With them, a thin line appeared. Nathan desperately focused on what he was seeing. It grew, changing from a curved line to the silhouette of a man. There was no face, just a hint from the outline that the man wore a suit. The silhouette walked towards Nathan, slowly. He was walking in place, moving forward every few steps, rather than every step.

One last click, then, in an instant the man was cut away by a booming sound that shook Nathan to his core.

-YAHWEY-

With the sound came flashes of images. Images Nathan had never seen before. He saw himself crying, sitting with his back to a fence. Then lifting logs onto a truck, followed by him having drinks at a bar with strangers who he treated like friends. He saw Vivian's face smiling at him. Then he was alone in the woods, looking at a tree limb that was floating in the air. It flashed away to both Vivian and him riding motorcycles together down a vacant highway in the sunset. He was happy, and so was she, but she looked worried. And as quickly as it came, it was gone, and Nathan jolted awake.

He caught his breath and settled. Laying in his bed he stared at the ceiling, feeling jarred from the experience.

"Oh, what was that?" he whispered to himself.

He had a tendency to speak to himself. He also had a tendency to shut things out because of his sensitive nature, which made the dream all that more jarring. After sitting up slowly and giving himself time to properly wake up, he turned on the lamp by his bed which gave light to his room. A showcase of his drawings and paintings hung from the walls. He stretched every muscle with a silent yawn. It was still early in the morning, and his two parents and older brother were fast asleep. Nathan slid to his bedside and walked over to his desk. It was the same action he performed countless times. Day in and day out he would sit at his desk and open his laptop. Once in a blue moon he would try to draw something, but he couldn't remember the last time he tried; a year maybe? He would mostly just browse the internet until his parents woke up. Though, for the last three months since March break, Nathan got into the habit of early morning bike rides to the Tim Hortons near his house. Vivian started working nightshifts there, and although Nathan wasn't a fan of coffee, he thought it couldn't hurt. The small action of buying a medium double double to put a smile on her face was worth it. Nathan didn't have the courage to talk to her, but the coffee was enough. However, this morning was different. Very different. That was no ordinary dream. The feeling left a mark. Nathan opened his notebook. The first time he had done so in almost a year.

-17/06/25-

'In all my mind that my eyes can't hide is who I am when I'm awake, but something bigger is happening. I can feel it. Maybe it hasn't happened yet. Maybe it already has, or it's in the middle of happening…'

He sighed.

'I don't know. I had a weird dream, that's all.'

"Nathan…" came a whisper. A disembodied female's voice; the one from his dream. He couldn't remember what she said but he recalled her voice. Nathan frowned as he looked behind him. To his lack of surprise no one was there. He sat for a moment, comprehending what he heard. It definitely *was* the same voice from his dream.

He opened his laptop and searched on Google: auditory hallucinations. The results were as he suspected;

stating that hearing one or more talking voices may be associated with psychotic disorders, such as schizophrenia or mania. 'Maybe I'm still waking up.'

Though he knew better, Nathan couldn't shake the eerie feeling that he was being watched, so he decided to distract himself with videos on YouTube. His 'want to watch' home page was littered with conspiracy videos. Nathan clicked on one entitled, 'War Ships Captured by N.A.S.A. 6/24/17'. The video showed N.A.S.A. footage of distant meteorites on the edge of the solar system, with some individual voicing over the footage. "Is it really meteorites? Don't be fooled by N.A.S.A; a government owned agency whose main goal is to-" -click-

Nathan shut his laptop with a sigh and rubbed his temples with the base of his palms. "I gotta stop watching so many God damned conspiracy videos," he grumbled to himself.

\*

The sun had just started rising, giving colour to the morning clouds. Nathan fiddled with his iPod while biking down the familiar suburban streets he'd known his whole life. Today he planned to bike down the shores of Lake Ontario, rather than get coffee. He had a lot on his mind and bike rides to the lake always helped. Whether it was the cool breeze, or the sound of rippling waves, there was something about standing on the edge of that vast space spanning the horizon that filled Nathan with a beautiful sense of scale.

He finally chose the song. It was a remix of: *Etude*, by Nero. Nathan hadn't heard the song in a long time and thought it was a good fit. As the song played, he lightly closed his eyes as he whispered to himself,

"I go out, past the planets, the stars, Milky Way, Laniakea, the universe… I'm just looking at a quark... There's nowhere outside, no way out of existence."

Nathan's body was in auto pilot as he continued.

"Dear God, you are the universe, trapped inside yourself. A *Flying padre*, just a conscious entity made up of us, like brain cells are to a brain…"

As a kid, Nathan's imagination would take over sometimes. Grocery malls turned into battle grounds. Parks, into newly discovered planets.

Nathan biked on, and begun imagining himself flying upwards, through the clouds. He could see the clouds shoot past him, and the horizon bend as he left the atmosphere. He slung-shot outwards into space. The Earth disappeared and the Sun shrank. Then the Sun disappeared with the other stars. Orion's arm glowed in its brilliance, then shrank, giving way to the Milky Way. Further and further Nathan went, out into the grand cosmos. Galaxies became dots like stars, intermingling into the veins of Laniakea.

Nathan rode on one of its filaments, until he was the size of the supercluster itself. The farther out he flew, the dimmer it got. The superclusters bubbled and gave shape to the borders of the universe. Nathan's vision blurred as other spheres appeared in the darkness, followed by whizzing electrons. The electrons quickly shrank, giving way to atoms. Then atoms, to molecules. Molecules, to an optic nerve. Nathan rode the nerve, which connected to the macula of a retina. And out he rode, through the crystalline lens. His sight went black, then began to focus outwards, only to be looking at his own eyelid.

\*

Nathan sat with his eyes closed in a pew beside his

classmates, all in gowns, inside the Cathedral Basilica of Christ the King. It was their graduation ceremony.

"Nathan—Farrantino," said the master of ceremonies. He opened his eyes and stepped out of his pew. His mother, father, and brother were all standing in the back of the church. His brother was not thrilled in being there, but Nathan's parents were ecstatic. He walked down the aisle and his mother discretely snapped a picture with her iPhone seven-pro. Nathan shook hands with his principle whilst accepting his graduation certificate, and the photographer flashed a photo.

He walked down the aisle, then stopped where his math teacher was sitting. "Excuse me Mr. Campbell?"

"Yes, Nathan what is it?" Mr. Campbell whispered.

"Can you hold my certificate? I have a bathroom emergency."

"Yes yes, of course. But be quick!"

"I will! Thank you."

Nathan hurried down the aisle and snuck out of the room through a door on the left. Then, instead of turning down the stairs, Nathan took a right and left the building. It was a little windy outside but sunny. Vivian sat alone on the church steps, smoking a cigarette. The door behind Nathan closed, alerting Vivian of his presence. She turned her head to see him.

"Hey padre," she said with a smile. The sun made her squint. "I missed you this morning. Tying to cut coffee?"

Nathan made his way to the steps and leaned on one of the railings. "Vivian missed me," he said, trying to sound cool. "I'm honoured."

She responded back sarcastically, "Yeah Nathaniel, Vivian missed you."

He smirked, but underneath was a bigger smile. "But no... You sittin' out here alone?"

"Not anymore."

She patted the concrete beside her. Nathan huffed a grin and sat down beside her.

"Not a fan of the church?" he said with a head nudge at the building.

"I have nothing against it... Are you catholic?"

"Yeah I mean," he shrugged, "born and raised."

"But are *you* catholic?" she asked.

"Well, the church is an institution, like any other. Rules change all the time. The bible's been translated and rewritten so many times... who really knows what happened two-thousand-odd years ago?"

"Do you believe in Jesus?" she asked with a chuckle.

"I believe in Jesus as much as I believe in Shakespeare. Did they really exist? It's all in speculation. And if they did, did they really do everything everyone says they did? We can never really know."

"So, what do *you* believe in, then?" Vivian asked.

"Ummm," Nathan laughed to himself. He was beyond nervous but figured if he didn't dive into it, he would have nothing else to say. "I like to believe in the idea of a cosmic-consciousness. I mean not literally but just the vague idea that like- the universe is God! Like, take our brains for example. It's made up of millions and millions of brain cells. They work really hard, and collectively they all make up us. You, Vivian. Me, Nathan. Now, you look at the whole universe, and collectively, we all make up this one, single, thing."

"It's not the same thing, though," Vivian retorted.

"Oh, no. The universe is a lot more complicated, with the whole eleven dimensions thing. We're three-dimensional creatures living in a linear path through time; which kind-of takes away from the whole free will thing Catholicism teaches us-"

"Wait, I don't know about that. How don't we have free will?" Vivian asked in a trance.

"Well think about it: can you change the laws of physics? Go back in time? If you can please tell me 'cause that would be awesome, but usually the answer is no. Since you can't change the laws of physics, and you can't go back in time, all you're really doing is reacting to the circumstances around you and making choices based off past experiences you had. It's like being offered three flavours of ice-cream. You can choose whichever of the three you want, but you'll usually go for the chocolate because your brain tells you you want it. Or the vanilla, or… yeah."

Vivian chuckled, and Nathan kept going. He naively felt like he was on a role.

"And we only have those three options. Imagine if you could have every flavour that ever existed, and even the ones that didn't. And your brain wasn't pulling you in one direction. That would be awesome."

She smiled, then looked at him more intently. "We've honestly never really talked before, have we?"

"No, not really."

They both smiled, giving Nathan butterflies. Vivian took a pull from her cigarette. "Do you have any plans tonight?" she asked.

Nathan shook his head with anticipation.

"You should come to Shawn's! He's having a party."

"Yeah! Umm, sure."

He tried to hold himself back from seeming overexcited but failed. It made her smile. She couldn't stop looking at him, which caused Nate's gut to twist in a knot. She took one last pull, then flicked her cigarette away. The two of them stood up, and Vivian extended her hand. "Call me V."

"Okay," said Nathan. He shook her hand, and she pulled it in. It surprised him, but he played along. She pulled a pen from her gown and started writing on his hand.

"This is Shawn's address," she said.

"Thanks… You uh, you know, it's the weirdest thing, but I actually had a dream about you last night."

V looked up at him, intrigued. "Oh?" she said with a raised eyebrow.

"Yeah it was really weird. You and I were riding motorcycles together on the highway. We were on our way somewhere but, that's all I remember."

"Do you ride?" she asked, excited.

It sounded like a joke to him. "No," he said with a shake of his head. "Do you?"

"No."

"Oh."

"Well we should get back inside," V concluded.

"Yeah, yeah," said Nathan.

The two walked back to the door, and Nathan opened it for V.

"Oh, thank you." She walked back into the church, then turned around. "So, I'll see you tonight?"

He smiled wide. "Yeah. For sure."

Nathan's excited attitude made V giggle. "Okay," she said, then hurried in.

\*

# Chapter Two:
## ~House Party~

The sound of a car turning down Nate's street let him know that his mother had returned from dropping his father off at the airport. The hour had struck nine in the evening and Nathan was rummaging through his parent's closet, looking for something cool to wear for the party. He pulled out his father's brown leather jacket, feeling satisfied that it would complement his attire. As Nathan tried it on, his mother called from downstairs to him. "Honey?"

"Yeah?" he asked.

"Is your brother still home?"

"No, he left as soon as you and dad did."

She paused for a moment to take into account where her son's voice was coming from. "What are you up to?" she asked.

"Is it okay if I take dad's brown jacket?"

"Sure, but what for?"

"I'm heading out."

"Oh! Where are you going?"

Nathan walked to his room and grabbed his notebook and iPod. Then he hurried downstairs, where his mom just started watching television. "Nathan?"

He stopped at the front door and turned around. "Yeah mom?"

"Where are you going?" she reiterated.

"I got invited to a graduation party."

"Oh, that's wonderful!" she exclaimed. "Come here."

"It's already late," Nathan said as he walked over to his mom in the television room.

"Whose house is it?" she asked.

"You wouldn't know him; Shawn from school. I was

invited by a girl, V."

Her face lit up at Nathan's mention of a girl. "That's great sweetie! How come I've never met V? Is that short for Vivian?"

"Yeah, well I just started talking to her. I got to go mom. I'll see you later tonight."

He walked away, and out the front door. His mother called out to him as he left. "Okay have fun! Don't be back too late!"

"I won't!" Nathan called out as he shut the door. He walked down the front steps and onto the street, then pulled out his Samsung Galaxy S III and mapped the address.

The smart phone was a gift from his father back when it first came out, near Nathan's grade eight graduation. The phone however turned out to serve very little purpose. His parents asked him over the years if he wanted a new phone, but Nathan never used it for anything aside from texting or calling the two of them, so he felt there was no need.

The map loaded the address and route from his current location. 'Only a twenty-minute walk,' Nathan thought to himself. 'That's not bad.'

He pulled out his iPod, but this time he had one song in particular that he wanted to listen to. It was the song: *What a Difference a Day Makes*, by Dinah Washington. The song title itself fit how Nathan felt as he walked to Shawn's house. With each step, his attitude turned from excited to anxious.

'What the hell am I doing? No one there's going to know me. Jesus…' Nathan took a deep breath in order to stop himself from getting psyched out. 'You'll be fine, you'll be fine.'

The house was close; Nathan could hear it behind his music. He put his iPod away as he turned the street corner, and there it was. The party scene was laid out in front of him, making him stop for a moment to take in what he was walking into.

'They're animals, drinking openly as if we don't have laws against this kind of shit. Ugh, shut up! Be cool, be cool. Alright… It's all good.'

He took another deep breath, and marched forward.

Music was blaring out of the open front door. Red party cups and cigarette butts were spewed out across the front lawn as if the Greek god Dionysus decided to update his look. Nathan walked up the front lawn, passed his fellow graduates, and into the house. Low and behold, inside was significantly worse than out front. Nathan didn't know what to make of the insanity in front of him.

To his left was the living room, which had transformed into a chandelier tournament room combined with a sensual grinding room. To his right was the kitchen, then television room. Both were overly crowded with people, who were either stuck or desperately trying to get somewhere. The music was deafening, and people talking above the music didn't help.

Nathan backed up against the wall at the entrance of the kitchen. He had no idea what to do, so he just stood there. Then, to his surprise, Ryan from his gym class shimmied over to him. "Hey Nathan! What's up man?!" he said, surprised to see him.

"Hey Ryan! Nothin'," said Nathan, trying to sound cool. "You?"

"Uh, nothing too. You want a beer, or anything?" he asked in a sincere voice.

"…Yeah, sure," said Nathan, trying his best to seem uninterested.

Ryan pointed to the fridge, saying, "I got the Molson in the fridge, if you want to grab us one each."

"Sure, thanks," said Nathan. He walked into the

crowd and began shimmying his way to the fridge. Ryan took Nathan's spot on the wall and waited for him there.

"Sorry. Excuse me," Nathan said as he shimmied. He got to the fridge and opened it up. In front view sat a fifteen pack of Molson Canadian beer, with a few missing. He grabbed two beers and shut the fridge behind him. As he prepared to enter the crowd again for his voyage back to the wall, someone he never met before stood staring at him. "...Hey," said Nathan.

"Hey, you enjoying the party?" asked the stranger.

"Uh, yeah, you?"

The man shrugged. "What the fuck are you doing with my FUCKIN' beer?"

Nathan's heart sank, and he became silent in confusion and fear. He looked over to where Ryan was, but he was gone. "What the fuck?!" the man yelled, stepping into Nathan's personal space.

"What?" Nathan spouted desperate confusion.

"Put my FUCKIN' beer down, dude! Come on," he spit as he grabbed Nathan by the jacket. Nate landed the beers on the kitchen counter just before being yanked and thrown before of the onlookers. They all moved out of the way and watched as the man pushed Nathan out the front door. Nate looked around frantically for help, but everyone that filed out behind him just formed a circle. The people wanted a fight.

""Fight! Fight! Fight! Fight!""

"Yeet!"

"Awe shit son."

"Finally, somethin'."

Everyone was shouting at once.

"Please... don't do this," Nathan whispered to the man, who did nothing but laugh at him. People from the crowd laughed too.

"Fuckin' worrrrld you think we live in, man?" Then in the blink of an eye, he punched Nathan in the face with notably resounding impact. Nate stumbled but somehow kept his footing. It surprised everyone, including the stranger looking up from his fist as he clenched and unclenched. Not knowing what to do, Nate burst into a sprint at the man in hopes that it would throw him off. He lunged at him and attempted a headlock. The struggle lasted seconds before Nathan's feet were kicked from under him, smacking him on the ground. The crowd exploded with roars. Then to everyone's terrible surprise the man began kicking Nathan as he lay curled on the ground, scared and helpless. "Fuckin' stay down!! Fuckin' teach you a leason!!"

"That's not cool man!" someone shouted out, just as a kick landed in the back of Nathan's skull. People gasped in shock, and Nathan went limp.

The combatant took a few steps back. No one in the crowd moved. Nathan's eyelids fluttered, then burst open. His pupils dilated, shaking his vision. Time itself slowed down… The shaking settled to a hum, and Nathan bounced up, standing straight and staring at his opponent. He lost his footing for a moment then kept steady.

"Fuck him up Nathan!!" one of the graduates shouted.

Blood dripped from the back of Nate's skull, soaking into his hair. Out of fear, and hoping Nathan would back away, the opponent threw a punch. But Nathan was unflinching as he caught his fist, mid-fly. In the same instant, he flung a right jab right into the stranger's gut.

"Oh, shit!!" someone screamed.

The man collapsed backward, wind taken from his lungs. Nathan's heart was beating at a mile-a-minute. His senses were numb.

"Fuckin' stay down," he said.

The crowd burst into an uproar. The stranger crawled away from the crowd, bent over with his arms around his abdomen. Fight enthusiasts ran at Nathan and hoisted him in the air. His senses came back to him as his heartrate slowed, and his pupil's constricted.

"Nathaaaaaaaan Farrentino!!" Shawn screamed from the crowd. The people let Nathan down and Shawn ran at him. He lifted Nathan up with a bear hug.

"OH!" yelled Nathan in surprise, and Shawn put him back down.

"I didn't know you'd be here man! Holy shit that was fuckin' epic! I didn't know you could fight!" he spewed.

"Me neither," said Nathan in all honesty.

"I've never seen you out before man," said one graduate as he entered the conversation.

"Yeah, this is the first real party I've ever been to." Nathan relied.

"Wait- shit, you gotta get that checked out?" the graduate addressed to Nate's head wound.

"Oh," Nathan began as he touched the wound and saw blood on his fingers, "I... I don't feel faint so I don't think it's a concussion or anything."

"Hey hey, fight or flight; you fuckin' held your ground man. That was fuckin' awesome," said another graduate, giving Nathan a fist to bump.

"That guy was a fuckin' asshole anyway," said the first graduate, whose name was beyond Nathan.

"Hahaha, thanks," he said.

Shawn put his arm over Nathan's shoulder and started walking the two of them back inside.

"So, who are you here with anyway? If you don't mind me asking."

"V- I mean, no. She invited me," he replied, as

Shawn finished his tallboy can and tossed it.

"Oh! I didn't know you two knew each other," Shawn said as the two walked through the front door, and into the kitchen.

"Yeah, she started working at the Timmy's right by my house, so I've been seeing her there."

"Oh, you two are seeing each other?" asked Shawn.

"No no," said Nathan, feeling slightly embarrassed. "Just, costumer / server kind of thing."

"Haha okay."
Shawn grabbed the two beers Nathan was holding earlier and twisted them both open. They cheered and drank. Nathan was disgusted in the taste but held it in.

"Well she's in the back," said Shawn. He threw his arm over Nathan's shoulder again, and the two of them walked to the backyard. When they got there, someone called Shawn away, and away he went. Nathan stood outside of the sliding door, looking forward. On the other side of the yard stood V, smoking a cigarette and laughing with a small group of people. She was looking cool with her dark hair in a fishtail braid, swimming down her cardigan and ending at the top of her jeans. Under the cardigan she wore a pink shirt as usual. She must have had a bundle of them.

"I just heard it was Nathan in that fight!" A girl entering the conversation exclaimed to V and the others.

"What?!" burst V.

"And he kicked the shit out of the guy-"

"Speak of the devil," one guy in their group said. He nodded up to Nathan, and Nathan gave the group a wave. V flicked her cigarette away and ran to him. She was beyond excited to see that he came.

"Nathan!" V cried. She hugged him tight. Nathan was

overwhelmed with happiness, causing his hormones to make him slightly erect.

'Oh my God no!' Nathan screamed in his head. He focused hard on calming himself down as V pulled back. Luckily she didn't notice.

"I heard you got in a fight?!" V asked.

"Yeah," Nathan said with a chuckle.

"Are you okay?" she asked. Nathan was surprised at how concerned she was.

"I'll be fine," he said. The two looked at each other, and Nathan smiled. V felt goofy, but couldn't help looking back at him with a big grin.

"She's gonna fuck him up," said the one guy from the group. It was loud enough for V and Nathan to hear and it made her laugh. She bit her lip, and for some reason Nathan became very intimidated by her. She grabbed his hand and the two hurried inside.

The following hours were nothing short of a dream to Nate. He became the life of the party. V was wrapped around his arm, and the two were the talk of the night. V fed Nathan wager bombs, tequila shots and vodka shots. They played beer pong together, and to Nathan's surprise, he was a natural. The two found themselves outside and decided to join a bun circle. The joint was passed to V, who inhaled, then leaned in to Nathan and gave him a kiss. She exhaled into his mouth, and Nathan breathed in. He exhaled slowly, computing the fact that he just kissed her. V, the one girl in his entire life that he always wanted to kiss.

'But was it real?'

"Nathaaan!!" Shawn yelled from inside.

"Come on!" said V as she grabbed Nathan by the arm and hoisted him up.

"Thanks!" he called out to the group as the two left to

go back inside.

"Where- Nathan!" Shawn spouted. Nathan could easily tell that Shawn was wasted. Shawn stumbled over to the two of them and threw his arm over Nathan's shoulder, sandwiching Nathan between the two of them.

"Nathan, why aren't you fucked up yet?!"

"Hahaha, I don't know. Is it a thing where if it's the first time you drink, it has no effect?"

"That's weed man," slurred Shawn.

"Wait, this is your first time drinking, ever?" asked V.

"Well I've had wine with my parents-"

"That doesn't count!" yelled Shawn.

"Haha alright, I figured," laughed Nathan.

Nate, V, and Shawn filled three tall glass mugs with the remaining beer in the kitchen. The hour was late. The population had dropped from over fifty, to around fifteen. The three cheered their mugs, and poured the mixed beer down their hatches. Nathan cringed, and a shiver shot up his spine.

"How am I not fucked up right now?" Nathan said under the stinging sensation.

V looked to Shawn, who wasn't looking hot.

"I think, I gotta-"

He threw up in his mouth.

"Oh no." V grabbed Shawn and pulled him in to the sink. He leaned over and puked.

"Good call," said Nathan.

"Thanks," V said with a smirk. "Let's get him to bed."

"Wait!" Shawn implored.

"No Shawn, the night's over," said V.

"No I know. I'm saying," -hiccup- "that you guys should take my room. I wanna sleep on the sofa."

Nathan and V were shocked. Shawn slumped off on his own to the living room, which was a disaster, and collapsed on the sofa. The two looked at each other in an awkward silence.

"Wanna go outside?" asked Nathan.

"Okay," V said with a chuckle.

They walked outside to find the stoners gone, leaving the backyard to just the two of them. They walked to the opposing fence and leaned against it. V lit herself a cigarette, then motioned to Nathan if he wanted a pull. Nathan took the cigarette from her and looked at it. He placed it in between his lips, and inhaled the smoke into his mouth. He immediately coughed it out, making V laugh.

"It's not cigar. Watch."

V took the cigarette from him, and put it to her lips. She pulled on the cigarette, took the cigarette away, and inhaled the smoke straight into her lungs. "And exhale." she said. And she exhaled.

Nathan took the cigarette and tried again. He inhaled the smoke until it burned, then released the cigarette and inhaled the smoke into his lungs. "So that's smoking." he said calmly as he exhaled.

He gave the cigarette back to V, and looked up. V followed suit, and the two looked at the nighttime sky, diluted by the suburban light pollution.

"I don't know why," Nathan started, "but, I can't help looking to the stars, and getting consumed by the sense of infinity."

V looked at Nathan, and kissed him on the cheek. Nathan immediately followed that action by kissing her on the lips. She kissed him back, and they began to make out. Their tongues intermingled, and Nathan felt hot. He couldn't hold his erection back this time. V pulled back, and grabbed Nathan's hand. She led him back inside, and up the stairs.

'Oh my God, oh my God, oh my God…' Nathan couldn't think straight. He just followed V's lead.

She opened the door to Shawn's room and continued making out with Nathan as the two walked inside. She pushed him onto the bed, and turned around to close the door.

Nathan was in. In the moment. Nothing else existed. No thoughts entered his head. He leaned back and watched V as she turned around slowly. She stood for a moment in the dim lighting, with her eyes locked on Nathan's. He sat, staying silent. Music from downstairs played to them. It was the song: *Between The Raindrops*, by Lifehouse.

V slid her cardigan off and unbuttoned her jeans. She slipped her pants off slowly. Nathan slid his jacket off, and she walked over to him. The two swallowed each other's tongues again vigorously, and V stripped Nathan's shirt off. They giggled nervously to each other as he lifted her's off, and she unclipped her bra. She was breathing heavy now. Nathan kissed her cheek, then her neck. He worked his way down to her right breast. V held his head, and worked her fingers through his hair.

"I've wanted this for a long time, Nathan," she whispered.
Nathan looked up to her. "I've… never, done anything like this before," he admitted to her. 'Why did I just say that?!' he immediately thought, scolding himself.

V huffed a laugh, and kissed him. She already knew he was a virgin. "Neither have I," she whispered.
Nathan eyes widened. '…Oh shit…'
His heart was racing a jet plane. He held back from talking any more, and kissed her. They twisted positions, and V unbuckled his belt. He pulled his pants down along with his boxers. Next came V's lace-edged underwear. He kissed

her belly, and moved down as he pulled her underwear off. He slipped them off her feet, and looked up to her.

V lay naked on the bed waiting for him. He crawled up to her and hovered over her. Nathan knew he would never forget this moment for as long as he lived. V wanted Nathan as much as he wanted her, and though neither of them said it, they were both in love.

*

"So what are you going to do now that high school is done?" she asked him.
The two laid in bed, early in the morning. The party downstairs was dead, and the streets outside were silent. Nathan and V were very tired, but neither wanted to sleep. Nathan felt incredibly calm.

"I don't know. Time will tell," he replied.

"Aren't you worried?" she asked.

"A little, are you?" He had a strong feeling that she only asked because *she* was.

"Well, I love my parents to death… but I can't keep living in debt."

'Oh,' Nathan thought to himself, piecing the puzzle of her employment.

"After summer I might disappear. Join a gang of drifters or something. And just, live… free."

Nathan could tell she meant every word. "Well until then just keep in mind that freedom is only a matter of perspective," Nathan said, hoping it might lighten her outlook.

"What do you mean?" she asked.

"Have you ever heard of the brain in the vat theory?" he asked. She shook her head.      "Well the theory suggests that right now, we're all just brains, floating in vats, and the world around us is a simulated reality."

V was silent for a moment. Maybe dozing off. "Then, what's real?" she asked.

He breathed in deep. "Who knows? Right now you could be in a simulation; without a body, or a brain. Just consciousness, and you'd never be any the wiser." he said with goofy tone at the end. He was now dozing off.

"Ooo," she said in a similarly goofy tone. Then she became serious. "You know… I've always had this strange sense of, uneasiness… Like I was missing something, or I didn't do something I should have; I don't know. But this feeling, it's been following me around for as long as I can remember. And being here, now, with you… It's just… gone."

Nathan took it in, feeling incredible.

"I love you, V," he said.

She was about to say the same thing… but then a curious look took her face. It confused him.

"What?" he asked.

"Your eyes…"

"What about my eyes?"

"…You have, a little diamond in your pupil." she said in a very sleepy, but astonished voice. She looked deep into his eyes. Into the strange diamond pattern, and further in, into blackness.

\*

The morning light shown in through Shawn's bedroom window.

"Nathan… Heed my voice…" came a whisper from inside Nathan that woke him up. His eyelids lifted and he sighed. The voice of the woman did not go away. V lay asleep in bed alone as Nathan walked over to the bedroom's bathroom to scrutinize his eyes. He leaned in to the mirror, trying to get the best view of his pupils. Upon close inspection he could actually see what V was talking about. It was faint, but he saw a shimmering translucent diamond shape, one tenth the size of his pupil.

"She must have had good lighting," he mumbled to himself. "First the dream and now this..."

He looked over to V and smiled before a familiar vibrating noise erupted from the bedside. Nathan walked over to his pants and pulled out his phone. He just missed a call from his mother. "Oh, right. Damn it," he breathed

Nathan clicked on the call history to call his mom back, and saw eleven missed calls from her. "What the hell?" he grumbled to himself.

He decided to get dressed, trying not to wake V, and call his mom back in the bathroom. It rang once, then when silent.

"Mom?" Nathan asked. "I'm sorry I didn't come back last night..."
He heard nothing on the other line. 'Why isn't she saying anything?!' he thought to himself.

Then he heard sobbing...

"...Nathan..." his mother quivered.

His heart quickened at the sound of her in distress.

"Mom. Mom what. What is it?" he said fast. "Mom..."

"It's your father sweetie..." she said with an unstable voice, clotted by her tears.

"Mom," said Nathan, sounding shaky. His eyes were swelling up. "What?.."

"His plane, crashed, last night..." she managed to utter. Nathan let out a gasp. He stared down at the unfamiliar counter top in front of him, and a tear escaped his eye. He began cry, deeply, into the phone. It was uncontrollable. Nathan loved his father so much. Though it would have shamed him to admit it, hearing the news from his distraught mother only grieved him further. His grip loosened, and he dropped his phone. The phone hit the ground, twisting and flipping from the reverberation.

"Nathan? Nathan?" his mother called out.

His insides were curling. Teardrops dripped on his phone, and V's eyes slowly lifted. She looked up to see Nathan, fully clothed, standing in-between rooms with his phone on the floor, and his wet eyes squeezed shut.

"Nathan?" V asked in a concerned voice. She was still waking up, and couldn't comprehend what was in front of her. Nathan rushed to the door and burst out of the room.

"Nathan?!" V called out. "Nathan!"
She threw the blanket off her and rushed out the room to follow him. Wearing only his shirt and her underwear, she chased after Nathan down the main stairs and out the front door. V ran down the driveway and looked left and right, but Nathan was gone.

"Nathan? Naathaaan!!" V called out. She was flustered with desperation and confusion, and then sadness. She slumped to her knees, and sobbed on the sidewalk.

Nathan had hidden away. His back was leaned against a fence on the corner of a nearby street. He slumped down and sat with his arms around his knees. Memories of his father began to rush through, bringing more tears. "Why?" he grumbled to himself.

A few moments passed, then he slid back up, wiped his face, and began to walk. He walked down the street, filled with heartache. He didn't know what he was doing but he kept walking.

'Run. Run,' Nathan thoughts told him. Just like that, he made up in his mind. He was going to disappear. He walked away, away from V, and his mother and brother.

'V! How could I do this?!' he thought to himself in absolute shame, but that same shame kept him from walking back.

As he walked, Nathan imagined himself floating upward again, into the beautiful spring morning clouds. He imagined floating away, and away he went…

*

# Chapter Three:
## ~Forty-Five Months, Twenty-Four Days~

Twelve, midnight. April nineteenth. Nathan was inside his head. He couldn't see a thing.

"Where am I?" he asked out to no one in particular. His voice echoed, and a blurry scene in front of him slowly focused. Through a summer haze he could see an empty hallway.

'But where? How did I get here?...' The hallway was very familiar. 'Wait a minute.'

Now he could see it. It was his old hallway. The same hallway he roamed his whole life until the day after graduation. He was confused as to why he was there, but at the same time couldn't help but silence the questioning and just soak in being back home. Down the hallway was his old room. He was seizing up inside from nostalgia as he gazed at the door. Void of a body left him unable to cry, or shout out. He wanted to walk inside but he couldn't move. Then the door opened. Two people came out with the sunlight behind them; a young man and young woman. They were running together playfully in slow-motion with sounds of people talking and birds chirping outside carrying on at normal speed.

It was him! The man was Nathan, and holding his hand was V. They were both dressed in colourful clothes. V wore a polka-dot summer dress and Nathan had beige shorts with a long sleeved plaid shirt. The true Nathan couldn't help his figurative heart from swelling up.

'Is this what could have been?' he thought to himself.

The sun caught his eye, and he found himself inside his room. Nathan and V were rolling around playfully on his bed, French kissing. As he watched, he began to hover

over them. Like the audience of a movie, he could only watch as a passive observer, going with the ride. His spirit halted over the *dream Nathan*, then floated downwards into his body. Everything went black, then his vision came back. He looked down at V with an absolute love in his heart, and she looked back at him with the same. Why it was happening was not relevant to Nathan. He never wanted the moment to end. But, just as that feeling filled him, V faded away.

"No, NO!" Nathan tried to scream in panic, but no sound came out.

His entire surrounding morphed around him, until he stood at the top of a ravine, looking down. He had his body now, but couldn't move. He looked around with his eyes to try and find out where he was, and it dawned on him. He was in his aunt and uncle's backyard. They always hosted thanksgiving, and Nathan loved to adventure into the ravine with two of his cousins that were his age.

"Why am I here?" Nathan tried to say out loud, with no success.

No one was going to answer him, he knew that much, but he couldn't help himself from asking. Then something caught his eye in the distance. At the bottom of the ravine, the ground began to cave in. It started small, but grew fast and stretched across the marsh lands. Was it an earthquake? He'd never actually seen an Earthquake before. It mesmerized him. The collapsing Earth travelled upward, on a course for Nathan. His heart pounded fast. He wanted to run. He tried desperately but his muscles wouldn't obey him. The void came, and swallowed him into its black abyss. The sensation of falling forced Nathan to tense up, which shot chills up his spine. The darkness didn't last long. A distant image came rushing up to fill Nathan's view.

He was holding V's hand, and the two of them were hurrying with an enormous crowd of people. Everyone was terrified. On the horizon of the flat, barren wasteland was a large structure. It was barrack-shaped, and seemed to be their destination.

"Wait!" V shouted in desperation to him.

He stopped and turned back to her. She was looking up. At the same time, a low hum boomed from above the thin clouds. Someone in the crowd screamed and everyone looked up. To all their horror, a giant foot came into view. It descended from above the sky, ripping the air under it to meet its victims. The building-sized, bone-looking foot had no toes, giving it the shape of a boot. It came down and crushed hundreds of the on lookers. The thousands that remained alive burst into panic. They scattered like ants. Nathan and V ran for their lives like everyone else, all towards the structure.

Nathan was pulled from his body, and he flew upwards at a tremendous speed. From a bird's eye view, he watched families and friends desperately sprint towards their only hope. Then more screaming erupted from hundreds more as a hand dropped a few kilometres to the right of the foot. Its six fingered palm smashed the ground, then scraped back like someone mushing bugs. Nathan continued flying out. There were two apocalyptic-looking titans. They stood over four kilometres tall, one with a hunch back and the other with horns. They were slow, considering their mass, but they covered a large amount of ground with each step.

Nathan's mind melted, along with his senses. When he came to he was hovering above his dream self once more. V was curled up next to him, and the two had their backs against a wall on the inside of the fortified structure. Debris fell from its high ceiling and everybody around them was hurrying in a panic. The two titans were smashing into the structure, wanting to get in. Get in to kill everyone. Survival was a bleak thought. The crowd's faith in making it through, was fleeting.

"Nathan..." the disembodied woman's voice called out.

There she was again. The faceless woman who only seems to exist in his dreams. Nathan's dream-self heard it too and looked up in confusion.

"This is what will come to pass if you cannot stop it," she said.

Dream Nathan tried to yell out in desperation but he had no voice. He looked around frantically and kept trying to yell out with no affect. He was scaring V more than she was already. The end was getting close for them. The structure was collapsing. Nathan watched on in horror, but he couldn't take anymore.

"Go. Let me go. I want to wake up! I want to go home!" he screamed.

The woman whispered to him but he couldn't make out what she was saying. Then without notice, everything quickly faded, ushering Nathan's wake.

His eyes lifted, and he couldn't help but stay still for a moment. He lay in his bed and stared at the ceiling, with his mind rushing over the highly vivid dream he just had. He drew a slow breath in through his nose, and out.

-BAGHH-

His alarm clock went off. He smacked the snooze button aggressively.

"Fuck!" He yelled to himself in angered confusion.

His reptilian brain kicked in however and he got out of bed. Normally his routine would follow with him brushing his teeth then getting dressed. However, he began scrounging through his dresser. Then his nightstand. He was looking for something.

The sun rose over the North Saskatchewan River and into his apartment window. His apartment, that looked as if someone just moved in. It was kept clean and held few things. He had the essentials like a fully stocked fridge and a well-kept bathroom, but he had no television or computer, just the alarm clock on his nightstand. All the walls were vacant of art, giving the apartment a dull feel. It gave Nathan the incentive to stay out as much as possible. Work would take up most of his daily life, but he still found time to go hiking, or during winter, use the Snap Fitness just south of his residence. He found that in the last year he was reading much more than he had ever before. He was mostly interested in the topic of philosophy, but found himself reading science fiction novels for the intrigue. On the weekends he would often go out and drink at bars with the intention of meeting strangers. Most of the time he would make friends with a group of people. He would tell them all about the one night that changed everything, and as the night would end, he would leave, never to see them again.

"Finally," Nathan said with satisfaction.

His old notebook; it was in the nightstand under the introductory paperwork for his current employment. He dove into his backpack to find a working pen.

-21/04/19-

'Spring again, a bitter-sweet promise, for better things that never come. Today is my "birthday", making this the year: twenty-twenty-one. I haven't written in this thing in a long time, but something's happened. After two years of not hearing any voices I had a dream again like the one from graduation, where I woke up wondering if what I saw was actually real... I can still hear the woman's voice. She said something-'

"Shit," Nathan said aloud. He thought about the dream long and hard, but it was already fading. 'What the fuck did she say? Ah shit.' he thought in frustration.

He tried to quote the mystery female, pausing at every punctuation.

'-something like: Save the man in flight, accept the killer's kiss... and, you will begin, or something along those lines. I don't know why it came back. I'm going to try harder to remember everything next time it happens and write it down. I have a strong feeling it means something. I mean it has to, I just don't know what. I don't know what to make of it, except that maybe I'm fucking insane.'

He dropped the pen on the paper, and closed the notebook. Nathan still had work to get to.

\*

The mornings were still cold, but the days were getting warmer. Nathan jogged down the staircase of his apartment, two stepping the way down to cut his time in half. The parking garage was his destination. It held his two-thousand-nine Nissan Altima, bought and paid for in cash as a Christmas present to himself back in twenty-nineteen.

The streets were waking up as Nathan rolled out. He listened to music from his old iPod. He wasn't doing it on purpose, but listening to that music was, in a way, trapping him in the past.

"Oh well," Nathan said with the song: *Back to The Shack*, by Weezer. "At least we raised some hell!"

He arrived at his employment: Arborlist, the first

name in tree care! Most people would simply nod and walk on as Nathan entered the workshop, but today was his birthday so he stashed his iPod away in a half-assed attempt to socialize on the off chance anyone might decide to talk to him. Phil, a short, older man with a pony tail, walked up to Nathan.

"Hey hey, happy birthday Al," he said with a grin as he gave Nathan's hand a shake.

"Amon! You're on beers today cause it's your birthday," shouted Nick from his bucket truck. Nathan didn't particularly like Nick all that much due to his overly rude attitude, and lack of intelligence.

"The fuck are you talkin' about Nick, it's Monday! I'll get Friday," Nathan shouted back to him.

"So, the double two! You got any plans after work?" Phil asked as the two of them walked into the shop.

"Not really. Probably go out for dinner or something like that."

"Yeah why not, heh heh."

He gave Nathan a nudge, and they walked their separate ways. Phil went to his locker, and Nathan to the main office doors where the groups of the day were posted on a white board.

'Oh fuck me,' Nathan thought to himself in disappointment. He was pinned with Richard, also known as Sudsy.

"You're with me Al," Sudsy called out to Nathan from down the hall.

"Yeah," Nathan called back.

"Well get a move on!" yelled Sudsy.

"We're both early as fuck Sudsy," Nathan retorted. Sudsy laughed and walked along to his locker. Nathan sighed, and walked over to his. He pulled his work boots out of his backpack and shoved it in his locker, along with his jacket and shoes. 'Another day,' Nathan thought to himself as he tied his bootlaces.

As the minutes passed, Nathan loaded Sudsy's truck with his gear. Two chainsaws, one blower, climbing gear, pole pruners, and the smaller stuff.

Nathan had been a grounds man at Arborlist for over a year, with more than enough of a skill set to manage a team himself. Mark: the district manager had offered him on more than one occasion a foreman's position, but Nathan declined. It paid better and held the same hours, but Nathan always felt that if he took the foremanship it would mean an end to his life. At least to the illusion of leaving. As a grounds man, raking leaves and pruning branches left the option for him to leave if he wanted to seek out another lifestyle.

He leaned against Sudsy's work truck and smoked a cigarette, watching as one by one, his co-workers made it in for the day. He waited there until everyone was present to perform the morning stretches.

"Oh-kay everybody!" Mark bellowed out to everybody outside the shop. "Time for stretch! Make a circle."

The team circled up and began stretches. Trunk rotations, advanced toe touch, thigh bend with ankle rotations, and wrist stretch were the important ones. Most people didn't go beyond that.

"Alright!" Mark yelled, "Now we all know with Derek gone we're going to need a new safety representative. So we'll be having a vote for that next Monday, okay? Those that want to run, put your name up on the board. In other news, it's Mr.Lurani's birthday today! Aye!"

Everyone clapped, prompting Nick to shout out, "Beers!"

People laughed, and Mark waved it off. "Okay, everyone have a good day today. Make sure to come back on time! I'm serious."

The group dispersed into their smaller groups of the day. Nathan hopped into the passenger seat of Sudsy's truck and waited for him. After a minute, Sudsy hopped in.

"You packed everything?" Sudsy asked.

"Yeah," Nathan responded.

"You got the poles?"

"Yeah I got everything," he specified.

"Alright," said Sudsy.

He started up the truck, and the two hit the road. Sudsy fiddled with the radio as he drove.

"Fuckin' news in the morning," he said as he changed the stations.

"Three ex-seafarers were found dead near-" one radio host said before cutting off. The next station was covering a bigger story, "-just released an announcement about the meteorites that were found by N.A.S.A. almost four years ago-"

Sudsy changed the station again. The next station was playing: *My God is The Sun*, by Queens of The Stone Age.

"Hey go back to the meteorites! I remember hearing about those," said Nathan.

"If I wanted lip from you Amon, I'd unzip my fly," said Sudsy. Nathan shook his head, which made Sudsy laugh.

"No you know what, fuck you I'm listening." Nathan switched the radio dial back to the news report.

"Hey! I'm the fuckin' foreman!"

"Shut the fuck up!" Nathan burst at him as he turned the volume up. Sudsy as shocked. Nathan never really acted like that before. He usually kept quiet, and so Sudsy did nothing.

"-was estimated to have taken the barrage of meteorites another few *years* before they potentially impacted the Earth, but that number has now been shrunk to only a matter of five to six months. We urge those listening to keep up to date with your local news to find out if you might need to head south, or if you will be safe, just by bunkering underground."

Nathan listened intently as they rolled into the nearby plaza for morning coffee.

"What the fuck does that mean?" Nathan asked himself.

"Doesn't mean shit. N.A.S.A.'ll do what N.A.S.A. does and blow them all up. I'm not going anywhere," Sudsy responded.

Another three Arborlist trucks came in behind them as Sudsy parked his truck and got out. Nathan jumped out of the truck and hurried to the Tim Hortons. He got there first, but a line was already formed. His co-workers Rae, who was known as the stoner, Kevin who was the youngest, and Danny who was known as the shortest came in behind him.

"What do you guys got today?" Nathan asked.

"Kevin and I got a double ash removal, then pruning for the rest of the day," said Rae.

"You're fuckin' lucky," said Danny. "Cause Hall didn't show up, so now I'm with Nick and Chris, bunch of fuckin' idiots."

Kevin laughed. "What about you?" Rae asked Nathan.

"Ah, gardening," shrugged Nathan. "I don't know, it's Sudsy so it should be an easy day."

The line moved forward. "Depends on what you mean by 'easy'," said Kevin. "Sudsy's a fuckin' dick hole."

Nathan reached the front of the line for ordering. "Hi

there, how may I help you?" said a very young-looking Asian girl.

"Hey, yeah. Can I get a large French vanilla please?" asked Nathan.

"I don't know, can you?" replied the girl. It caught Nathan off guard and the girl laughed.

"Sorry," he said with a laugh. "May I?"

"Yes, of course," the girl said with a grin. She turned around and prepared Nathan's beverage. It was the smallest thing, but for the first time in a long time, Nathan felt happy. She turned back to him with the cappuccino in hand.

"That'll be three, sixty," said the girl.
Nathan pulled out the appropriate change from his wallet and gave it to her. When the girl reached out to accept the money, Nathan saw faint cut marks across her wrist.

'What?.. Why?..' he thought to himself. His chipper mood dropped as he walked away, and into a melancholy reflection on his own self.

'Shit,' he thought. 'There goes... no, shut up. You're good. It's all good.' He tried his best to shake it off.

Nathan and Sudsy got back on the road. They both lit cigarettes and smoked in silence. Nathan held the cigarette with the filter sticking out from his palm rather than the tobacco. It was his way of smoking discretely. Sudsy put his cigarette out on the floor of the truck and put the butt in his pocket as they came to a red light. In the right-hand lane a police cruiser rolled up next to their truck. Nathan was in the middle of taking a pull as it happened. In shock, he put the cigarette out on the door and held his breath. Sudsy looked forward, but had his sight pinned on Nathan.

"Don't do it," he said to Nathan, who was struggling to hold his breath. "Don't fuckin' do it Al. Hold it in."

Nathan's face was going red. In an act of desperation, he swallowed the smoke, and gasped for air.

"Uegh!" blurted Nathan in disgust. The light turned green, and the cop drove on. Sudsy laughed hysterically as Nathan rummaged through his lunch bag for a Gatorade. He gulped down half of a bottle and sat back to catch his breath.

"Alright Al," said Sudsy as he turned a corner "the number's four-one-one-four."

"Kay," Nathan said as he sat up.

The address numbers dropped as they drove. Four-one-five-oh. Four-one-three-two.

"Up ahead," he said.

They stopped at their address, and Nathan began procedure. He opened the truck's side bin and pulled out road signs for men at work.

"Get the yield too," Sudsy yelled from the truck. Sudsy took his sweet time writing the work order before he got out and walked up to the house. Nathan flung the pylons out, and jumped in the back of the truck for the wheel barrel, rakes and shovel. After talking to the client, Sudsy walked back to the truck and bellowed, "Rigging bag Nathan."

"Can't even form sentences, non-the-less have manners. Fuckin' red neck retard. Pull your own weight, fat ass," Nathan whispered to himself under his breath.

He climbed out from the back and opened up the side bin again, grabbed the rigging bag and walked it to the base of the metasequoia glyptostroboides, located in the front lawn.

"Hey," Nathan asked, "what tree is this?"

Sudsy walked up to him with a lit cigarette in his mouth, while strapping his helmet on. "How long have you worked here, Al?" he said, putting his hands on his hips.

Nathan knew it was a rhetorical question meant only

to insult him, but he answered in spite. "Almost a year now actually."

Sudsy walked away, then called out to him, "It's a 'DAWN REDWOOD'…"
DAWN REDWOOD… the words paralyzed Nathan. His vision shook, and he felt fuzzy.

"Amon!" Sudsy yelled at him. Nathan blinked, and he was holding a rigging line under the tree, with all his equipment on. Sudsy stood fifty feet over him in the tree.

"Uh, sorry," said Nathan. 'What the fuck just happened?'

"Focus!" Sudsy yelled.

Nathan pulled the rope tight. "Kay," he yelled up to him.
Sudsy revved his chainsaw, and severed a tree limb attached to the other side of Nathan's rope. Nathan lowered the limb and untied the knot. He put an eight-figure in the rope and pulled it up to where Sudsy tied a block. The knot hit the block, and Sudsy reached for it with his hand saw, but the rope was just out of reach. He unclipped his life line and stepped onto a closer branch. Sudsy caught the rope, and his secondary line snapped. He fell forward. Nathan watched as Sudsy free fell from the dawn redwood. And like being kicked in the back of the head, Nathan's pupils dilated. Time slowed. Nathan ripped the grass from under his foot as he burst into a sprint. He dove forwards, and Sudsy landed in his arms. Time kicked back and Nathan tumbled Sudsy away from the falling branches. He broke old Sudsy's ribs, and winded him, but he was alive. The two lay on the ground, Nathan panting, and Sudsy in shock.

"Aehl, Aheeh."

Sudsy was trying to say something but didn't have the breath for it. Nathan sat up and looked down at him. He was pointing to the truck. Then it made sense.

"Oh right!" Nathan yelled.

He ran to the truck and grabbed his phone. 9-1-1. The phone rang, and Nathan looked over to Sudsy, to see if he was still breathing.

'Still breathing.'

*

# Chapter Four:
## ~The Bar~

The bubbly tide came in, and went out. Came in, and went out. Nathan tilted his pint glass left and right, and watched the suds slide down. He looked to the bar and took a sip. Three of his co-workers walked up to him with pints in hand, and sat in the vacant seats surrounding him. Jim, Rae, and Danny. Jim sat tall, with a long orange beard. He was the true definition of a lumber-man in Nathan's opinion. His hairy hand pushed a shot to Nathan.

"This one's for you bud. For your birthday, but more importantly, for saving Sudsy's life."

"Thanks Jim," said Nathan. "What's in it?"

"Ginger blood," said Jim, who wasn't interested in questions.

"Whuhuat?"

Jim was one of the funniest men Nathan knew. His big beard, rosy cheeks, and cartoon voice made everything he said hysterical.

"Just take it. Cheers!" cried Jim.

They took the shot together, and Nathan coughed. They all laughed.

"That was fuckin' hot!" Nathan said with his eyes squinted. He took a swig of his beer to drown the taste.

"Can I just be the first to say that Sudsy should be fuckin' dead?! Danny blurted.

"Yeahh, Sudsy's fuckin' reckless in a tree," said Jim.

"No but I mean-"

"If someone else was his grounds man, he'd be dead," Rae said to conclude Danny.

"Yeah," said Danny.

"How the fuck'd you even pull that off Al? You just

superman tackled him mid fall?" asked Jim. Nathan laughed.

"Yeah I don't know. Reflexes I guess."

"Well shit, I want some of that reflex," said Jim.

They all laughed and continued conversation, but Nathan's attention drew to the front doors of the bar. A group of punks entered. Three guys and a girl. They were dressed in what looked like road warrior outfits, with leather jackets and torn jeans. The tallest guy had bleached blonde hair, which Nathan thought was a little weird. But the girl... the girl was...

'V!'

Nathan's eyes widened. He quickly turned his head in panic. "Hey Rae,"

"Yeah?"

"Wanna go for a smoke?" Nathan asked.

"Yeah sure."

Nathan and Rae walked to the back of the bar, and went out the other entrance.

Danny took a sip of beer.

"So Dan, you hear about those seafarers found dead?" asked Jim.

"Huh?"

Rae and Nathan lit their cigarettes under the dim orange glow of the back bar light.

"So, you have a brother, you said, right?" asked Rae.

"Yeah, yeah," said Nathan.

"Is he like you at all?" asked Rae.

"No, actually. He's like the opposite of me; into sports and that shit. You guys'd like him. My whole family's pretty normal. I'm just like the weird one out," said Nathan in a lighthearted tone.

Rae looked like he was going to say something back, but fell short, and took a pull instead.

"I know I'm weird. It's fine. I kinda like it."

"Don't worry about it Al. Honestly, everyone who works here is fuckin' weird, one way or another. They just hide it by pretending to be *all tough* all the time. They put up a show, but it's all bullshit... Even though you're a little quiet,"

"Yeah," Nathan said, huffing a laugh.

"You're like the only guy here who doesn't actually hide who you really are. You know?"

"Yeah I think I get it. Thanks," said Nathan. He flicked his butt, and Rae flicked his.

"You're cool too," Nathan said as they walked to the door.

Rae and Nathan entered the bar and sat back down with Jim and Danny. V was still there, playing pool with her gang. She didn't seem too interested on Nathan's side of the bar.

"Remember when he fell like, fifteen feet from that spruce a few years ago?" asked Jim.

"Man he just fuckin' hit the ground and rolled. He was lucky that ground was slanted," spat Danny.

"The way he treats our protocols, something like this was just a matter of time," said Rae.

"And you know he was thinking of Paul too, when he fell," Danny continued.

"Is that why he's always so bitter?" asked Nathan.

"Well you'd be too. I mean, fuck," said Jim.

"It's like dirty laundry," said Nathan.

"What? How's it like dirty laundry?" asked Danny.

"Well that's the way I see it with grief. It's like dirty laundry, cause, you either take it out and move on, or live with the stench. My dad, actually died a few years ago... so

I know what it's like."

Everyone was silent and attentive as Nathan continued. "It'd just kill me to see Sudsy go through that for the rest of his life, you know?"

"Shit yeah I know man," said Jim. "It's been six years and he still hasn't been the same."
V was on the move. The oldest-looking guy of the group went with her out the bar, and Nathan started tapping his right heel.

"C'mon let's change the fuckin' subject," said Danny.

"Sudsy was saved today, that's all that matters." Rae addressed to his beer.
Nathan couldn't hold it back. He had to do something. "I'll be back in a minute," he said, and left the group.

Nathan exited through the back door and held it as it closed. Slowly, quietly. Flames danced in the cup of his hand as he lit yet another cigarette. He let the smoke drag out of him, then he blew it away. "Okay hotshot, what's the plan?"

Nathan groaned at himself for not growing a backbone. Listening in on her conversation seemed to be a safe option, so he chose that. The sound of the bar light buzzing drowned out Nathan's footsteps as he crept to the corner of the building. The song: *Seasons*, by Future Islands played in the background.

"Yeah I know hahaha," V's acquaintance said. "I'm still shit."

"Eh, better for me haha."

Ah, V's voice. It'd been so long. It felt like drugs to Nathan. As soon as he heard her, he wanted to jump out from behind the wall and run to her, but saner thoughts prevailed. Cigarette butts hit the ground and footsteps to the bar crunched and scraped. The man turned around.

"You comin' in?" he asked.

"In a minute," V replied.

"What's up?"

"Nothing. Just be in in a minute."

"Okay," said the man, confused.

Nathan listened to the bar doors open and close. 'Now's your chance.'

V lit another cigarette.

'Take it or leave it.'

Nathan took a long pull, and exhaled. He bounced off the wall with casual grace and turned the corner. V's head snapped to him like a cat. She looked surprised and not surprised at the same time. Nathan walked over to her. The two looked at each other in a trance, and the wind spoke for them as they both soaked each other in.

"Been a long time…" said Nathan.

V nodded. "Mhmm."

"I… I, uh…" Nathan lost it; whatever cool he had. His quivering lip made him lower his head. "I'm sorry."

"Your Dad died…" V said sympathetically. "Then your Mom and brother, I don't know how I'd-"

"W-wait what?! What the fuck do you mean my Mom and brother?" Nathan said in a panic.

V let out a gasp. "You didn't know? Your, house… it caught fire the night you disappeared."

Nathan's emotions boiled. His insides were blistering. "What? What?"

V couldn't hold herself back from crying. She held her mouth and sobbed. Nathan turned away from her as he began to hyperventilate. Tears flooded from their ducts and Nathan grabbed his head.

"You're-" he managed to whimper before sucking in a quick breath. "-Telling me, my whole family's fucking dead?!"

V "…What are you gonna do?" she said with an inside voice under her tears. "Are you gonna run away again?"

That hit Nathan hard. As he caught his breath his eyes widened in shock from her comment. Being beyond the point of feeling embarrassed, he turned around to face her. He let his breathing slow down as he composed himself enough to slowly shake his head at her. She walked over to him and hugged him hard. She left an imprint of her face with mucus and tears on his jacket. He didn't mind.

Nathan wiped his face and nodded. "It's good to see you again."

"You to," said V. She smiled at him, then said, "Umh, Shawn's having another party. It's this Saturday. Last time I talked to him was months ago, but he said it'll be small, just old friends; some new."

"I barely knew him," Nathan said.

"He'd want to see you."

V walked to the door, then looked back at him with a smile, and went inside.

"Has he moved?" Nathan called out to her. He waited a moment, but got no reply.

The bar door looked like a mouth that swallowed V whole. Nathan backed up, then turned around and walked his way to the back door. As he turned the corner his co-workers exited the bar.

"Hey what happened to you? Drop your lollipop?" Jim joked.

"We're heading out?" Nathan asked them.

"Yeah, we got work tomorrow," said Danny.

"But I haven't paid yet."

"Don't worry about it, I got you," said Rae.

"And the taxi's here," Jim added.

He walked with them to the edge of the parking lot where a

taxi rolled in. They all loaded themselves into it. Jim in the front, and the rest in the back. Danny was the smallest so he sat in the middle.

"You'll be hitting fifty-one street for me, sir!" Jim told the taxi man.

They rolled out of the parking lot and onto the empty street. Nathan looked back at the bar as they left, and saw V's gang filing out. The sounds of their engines roared in the quiet night, causing Nathan's co-workers to look back with him.

"Whussat?" burbled Jim.

"Never seen a bike gang here before," admitted Rae.

The gang roared past the taxi, riding dangerously close. V had the rear and was approaching quick. Nathan didn't know what to expect from her. He hadn't got the chance to fully know her in the past, but he could tell how different she was now.

V closed in to the taxi's rear right window, where Nathan sat, and slapped a ripped piece of paper onto it. The paper stuck with chewed gum and read: YES. She smiled at him, then sped away, up to her gang and into the empty night. Nathan sat with his heart on fire. Life was brought back into him, and in a way he would never have expected.

The arborists all howled to each other as Nathan sat silently, with a smirk on his face.

"YES? What the fuck is yes?" asked Danny.

"What the fuck was that?" asked Rae

"Hahaha, cool," said Jim

"What was that about?" Rae continued.

"What'd you do Al?!" Shouted Danny.

"Ahahaha! Ah that's hilarious, Al's gonna join a bike gang and become her slave," Jim said to his co-workers.

Nathan took a breath. "Yeah, I know that girl."

"So what's yes?" Danny asked again.

"Looks like I got plans this weekend," said Nathan.

Rae and Jim shouted. Nathan looked at the taxi man, who was straight-faced and terrified as he drove.

Danny had a huge grin on his face. "You crazy motherfucker. Who knew Al had it in him?"

"I didn't question his silence for a minute," said Rae.

The taxi veered right on the road, and drove off, like the bikers, into the empty night.

\*

# Chapter Five:
## ~A Long Time~

Sunrise replaced the night, like a sheet of cashmere being replaced with sandpaper. It woke Nathan quite rudely, as he was in the midst of dreaming up V. She was in his arms, back at his house. It was a dream, he now knew, never to come true.

The day was Tuesday, only Tuesday. The week was the seventeenth. A week that was to be remembered by Nathan as one of the longest weeks in his life.

Tuesday April twentieth, twenty-twenty-one. Nathan worked with Jim on an ash tree removal.

"Look at this fuck off tree," said Jim as they walked their gear up to the fuck-off tree. "Well, you know what they say, it's not a mirror so quit fuckin' lookin' at it."

It was a very large, very dead tree.

"Four days, fourteen hours," Nathan whispered to himself.

Wednesday April twenty-first, twenty-twenty-one. Nathan worked with Danny.

"Alright, let's do this," said Danny. Nathan and Danny clunked out of the truck and grabbed their equipment.

Thursday April twenty-second, twenty-twenty-one. Nathan worked with Jim again. All the while on the side of his work, Nathan was also paying close attention to the radio news. To the point where everyone else at work was too. They took interest but did not nearly care as much as he did.

His face was red hot and dripping with sweat as he hauled a large bundle of branches behind him through a client's fence door, and down the driveway. The roaring sound of their chipper drowned out most noise. Jim stood by the mechanical beast and watched Nathan as he came into view.

"Oh fuck yeah bud!" the bearded ginger shouted. "Is that the last of it?!"

"Yeah!" shouted Nathan.

Friday April twenty-third, twenty-twenty-one. Nathan didn't know it yet, but that day was to be his last as an arborist. He was working with Rae. The two of them sat in the truck at the beginning of the day, going over their work order.

"Yeahhh, we got an easy day today," said Rae.

"Alright, awesome."

The day slung itself on Nathan as dead weight while he worked. He pruned, clipped, dragged, and cleaned. Before he knew it, the work day was over. The week ended. Nathan sat down at a collection of benches and chairs, all in a circle beside the workshop. He pulled out his cigarettes and his iPod from his backpack. He fingered each earbud into his ears and scrolled down his playlist menu. Rock, no. Indie, no. Slow, no. Classical, yes. He selected the song: *Arabesque One*, by Debussy, and it began to play.

Nathan lit a cigarette, and watched the embers burn; scrutinizing the direction of the burning as the wind blew. Then his co-workers appeared, all taking seats and beers. Nathan yanked his earbuds out and grabbed a beer with them.

"Nathan the meteor man!" Jim declared. "Leaving us to save more lives and make love to motorcycle chicks."

Everybody laughed.

\*

Nathan hadn't anticipated the duration of the drive. He only stopped twice for gas, food, and bathroom breaks. Burlington was three more hours away, on top of the twenty-six hours he had already been driving. The sun sank for the second time now as he drove, being replaced by street lights. City names he knew flew by as he continued southward. Then he saw it. Lake Ontario. It looked like home. Shortly after came his actual hometown. It'd been a long time since he saw the familiar streets and shops. Nostalgia was fogging his windshield.

After one last washroom break at a gas station, (where the man behind the counter watched on his phone updates on the meteorites,) Nathan parked his car. He decided to park it in the old Tim Horton's plaza near his house, and walk to Shawn's. He locked his car and started his journey down memory lane. Walking down the same streets he knew as a child after it had been so long acted like a drug to him. They shot him up with lost memories, numbing his senses.

He passed the park where he made his first friend, Jasmine. They were three, and they both liked ladybugs.

'What ever happened to her?' he thought.

The walking continued. His elementary school came up to him on his left. A life time of memories were encased within its five foot, chain-linked fence. Eight years there, eight long years. Full of development, friends, crushes, classes and holidays.

"Where did it all go? What did it accumulate to?" he asked himself.

The teachers, the students, the public speakers and church helpers. All of Nathan's childhood memories were like a fleeting dream to him. He felt their presence, but couldn't quite get to them.

Walking, walking, walking. Nathan knew what was

coming up. He couldn't distract himself anymore. The street he grew up on was nearing. Gravity increased the closer he got. And… His pace skipped a beat the moment he found himself walking past it. His house was the second on the right. It was covered by the first house, but not for long. The walking continued, then stopped. Nathan stood at the corner of the street looking downward at a house. It wasn't his house. It was strange, different than all the other houses on the street. Where was his home? It should have been right there but it wasn't. V wasn't lying. Grief got caught in Nathan's lungs. He could barely breathe. He had to keep walking, make it disappear.

The trek continued for twenty-six minutes until Nathan arrived at Shawn's house. It stood just as Nathan remembered it, but without the mess. He walked up the front lawn like last time but was stopped by the front door.

"Okay."

Nathan knocked on the door, and through the muffled conversations he could hear inside, a voice said, "hold on," and closed in. Shawn opened the door.

'He doesn't have short hair anymore.' Nathan thought. It was a strange thought but the first one that came to his mind.

"Nathan!!" screamed Shawn, with the familiar excited attitude Nathan remembered.

"Hey man," said Nathan with a grin.

Shawn grabbed Nathan and gave him hug.

"Man it's been too long, Jesus. Dude, you're jah-hah-hacked! How've you been?"

"I've been good," Nathan said with a chuckle. "Just been working labour."

"Oh yeah?"

"How about you?" asked Nathan.

"Yeah I've been good man, good. Been travelling a

lot. I just got back from California."

"Oh no way!"

"Yeah yeah, the beaches there, man; ah! But anyway c'mon in," Shawn said, gesturing Nathan inside. "You're a little early-"

"Really? What time is it? I thought I'd be late," said Nathan as he took his shoes off in the front hallway. The song: *Ruby*, by Twenty One Pilots was playing in the background.

"I don't know, eleven? Party's at twelve."

"Oh, okay."

"BUT, I was gonna say, guess who's already here."

Nathan held back from responding, catching that it was a rhetorical question, and grinned. Shawn was giddy for him; frivolous. The two of them walked together into the living room, and standing next to the sofa that Shawn passed out on four years ago, was V. She was talking to some guy Nathan vaguely remembered, and so he stood by the entrance. Shawn re-entered his old conversation with a tall, European-looking man. V looked to the entrance, at Nathan.

In Nathan's mind, he was in nirvana, a blissful star of relief. For three long years, Nathan was known to the public as Amon. Someone he was not. A hard man, good for cheap work. Nathan was always soulful and warm-hearted. He was a soft, kind, and scared boy. Now that he was home again, he was Nathan again.

V stopped her conversation with what's-his-name, and walked over to Nathan. "So you made it," she said.

"Yeah."

*

More people were arriving by the minute. Nathan and

V situated themselves on the sofa. They were deep in conversation.

"I still can't believe he shit himself in tenth grade," said Nathan.

"I always thought that was just a rumour!"

"No! I was in his class when it happened."

"Oh my God," V said through a fit of laughter. She settled herself, and Nathan felt the start of a new conversation begin.

"So what happened?" asked V in a lighthearted tone. "How did you end up so far away?"

"Well that's a big question. I guess the simple answer is: I walked, drove, got rides…" she nudged him. "As far as why that direction; this is gonna sound weird but, I felt like I was being pulled. Like a magnetic compass in my head was screaming, 'Go Northwest!' I don't know, heh. But what about you? Where'd you go? What'd you do?"

V looked down and cleared her throat.

"How'd you become part of a bike gang?" Nathan asked.

"I was expecting that question for a little while now, haha. Wellll- first off we're not really a gang, like hell's angels or red devils. We're rubber tramps. We live on the road. We're more like nomad punks. A family on wheels."

"Okay," said Nathan. He noticed Shawn walking up to them.

"It all started a month or so after graduation-"

"Heyyy Nathan and V," Shawn said, cutting into the conversation.

"Heyyy Shawn," V said, imitating Shawn's tone.

"Look at you two love birds catching up on lost time. C'mon, it's almost twelve. To my room!"

Nathan and V got up. "Why your room?" asked Nathan.

"You'll see."

Shawn grabbed Nathan's hand and started walking him away. Nathan grabbed V's hand and they all trained their way upstairs to Shawn's room.

"Okay, what's the surprise?" asked Nathan.

Shawn opened up his nightstand and pull out a bag of dried up mushrooms; psilocybin mushrooms.

"You guys ever do shrooms before?" Shawn asked them in his usual, excited voice.

""No,"" Nathan and V both said at once.

"Well what do you guys think?"

"Is that what everybody's doing at midnight?" asked V.

Shawn shrugged. "More or less."

V looked to Nathan, and Shawn looked to the both of them, eager for a response.

"Well? What do you guys think?"

"You wanna?" Nathan asked V.

"If you wanna."

They were both nervous.

"I'm running on like two nights with no sleep, is that gonna fuck me up?"

"Only in all the right ways," said Shawn.

"Ahh, hahaha." Nathan didn't know what to say. He gave V a look that said: why not?

"Okay let's do it!" yelled V with excitement.

"Yes!"

"Are we going to be fine, doing it for the first time at night?" asked Nathan.

"Yeah totally. As long as you're with the right people, that's all that matters."

"Okay."

Nathan and V were still nervous, but very, very excited. Shawn pulled three large mushrooms out of the bag and handed them out. He raised his mushroom, and the other two followed.

"Here's to a night, that we will never forget." Shawn toasted.

"Cheers!" yelled Nathan.

""Cheers!""

They tapped their shrooms together and chowed down.

"Make sure to chew it for as long as possible," Shawn mentioned.

They all made their way back down the stairs, and into to the party. The song: *Beast Infection*, by Grimes was playing. It filled the house with a mellow tone. Shawn raised a hand and proclaimed to the crowd, "Let the midnight party, begin!"

""Aye!"" the people cheered.

"The end of the world party!" someone else called out.

Some people already got started. Lincs were being chopped on the kitchen countertop, and microdots were being ingested. Shawn joined the group in the kitchen, and Nathan and V headed onward, to the backyard. He followed her out and shut the sliding door behind them, relieved to get away from the crowd.

"What the fuck," Nathan whispered to V. "Did you know Shawn got into psychedelics?"

"Yeah but I didn't know he got into cocaine," V said, discretely pointing inside.

"I don't think that's cocaine. If everyone here's planning on tripping out, it'd be K."

"What's K?" asked V.

"Ketamine. It's a horse tranquillizer."

"Oh."

Nathan pulled out two cigarettes and lit them both,

giving one to V.

"Here," he said.

"Thanks," said V, then continued after a drag, "I've never really been to a party like this before."

"Yeah me neither."

Shawn opened the sliding door. "Hey you guys can smoke in here," he said.

"Yeah? asked V.

"Yeah, my dad left about a year ago so it's just my mom and I, and we both smoke pot so it's cool."

"Oh, okay thanks. Sorry to hear about your dad man," said Nathan.

"It's okay- wait, Jesus. I completely forgot about what happened to you!" Shawn pulled Nathan in for another hug.

"It's okay. I'm alive, right?"

Nathan took comfort in Shawn's hug more than he put off.

"My condolences."

"Thanks," Nathan said with a smile. V took his hand and began walking him to the living room again. "We'll be on the sofa when you're done, Shawn," she called out.

"Okay, you two enjoy yourselves."

V took a seat. She looked a little bewildered.

"You feeling anything?" asked Nathan.

"I don't know… maybe? I think I feel something."

He took a seat next to her. "It'll probably take a while for me."

"Oh yeah?" V asked in a playful, fuck-you tone.

"Yeahaha."

"Oh yeah? Tough shit?"

"It's in my blood, on my dad's side. We Australians got poisoned so much we've become immune to it."

"You're Australian?!"

"Well my grandpa is."

"Oh I didn't know. That's cool."

"Yeah it's not bad. We can handle toxicants, but we don't seem to talk too much. At least not my grandpa and dad."

V sat silent, intent on Nathan continuing.

"I can remember one time," he blurted as the memory hit him, "where my dad actually pulled an amazing line. Like a heart to heart moment with me."

"What was it?" she asked.

"I must have been ten. Our dog Moe died and I hid away in my room cause I couldn't stop crying. And my dad, to my utter surprise, came in and told me, 'You know son, in life, the further you walk, the more you know. The more you know, the more you grow. The more you grow, the less you feel. And the less you feel, the further you walk.' At the time I just thought he was being a heartless asshole, but I see now what he meant. Life's taken my family away and yet... I'm not destroyed. I don't quite know how to say it but I feel as if, something might have played a role in my survival, so far. But then again, maybe not at all and it was just dumb luck. Who knows."

"Have I ever told you why I first started liking you?" she asked.

"...Was it my dashing good looks?"

V burst into laughter, but forced herself to stop. Her behavior was becoming noticeably different. "No! You acted different from everyone else, you still do." She caressed his face. "That's what I love about you. The fear to conform has never affected you. You're just you. You always have been... And your dashing good looks."

Nathan leaned in and kissed her, and his mind melted. He hadn't felt her lips in almost four years, making it ecstasy. They began to make out, and something started to change. Their senses tingled. They swapped saliva, and their tongues transformed. They became slugs in a mating ritual. In any normal circumstance, Nathan would have been creeped out beyond imagining and stopped, but it felt… strangely, right. After a minute, he pulled away. They looked at each other, and felt as if the world around them disappeared. It was pure bliss.

The european-looking man walked up to Shawn as he was making his way to the love birds.

"Shawn," he said, "we are going to go for a walk."

"Adventure away."

"We may not come back; you do not want to come with us?"

"I think I'll stay here with Nathan and Vivian."

The man understood, so he put his hand on Shawn's shoulder and said, "Ja rozumie." Then a girl walked up to them. She was short and had a big round head with long, bushy hair. "This is Karol with a K. She wants to stay too," he said.

"Nice to officially meet you, Karol with a K," said Shawn. He took her hand and gave it a kiss.

\*

Nathan walked out of Shawn's bathroom. The song: *Red Giant*, by Stellardrone was playing rather loud downstairs. It sounded like what music in space would sound like. Nathan didn't know if something was taking him over, but he walked over to Shawn's nightstand, and pulled out the bag of shrooms.

"Accept the killer's kiss…" he mumbled to himself.

He hesitated for a moment to make up his mind on what he should do, then scooped his hand in the bag and pulled out the bulk of the shrooms, and ate them. The music intensified. He chewed them into mush in his mouth, then swallowed, and down Nathan went. Down the stairs and back to the party that consisted of Shawn, V, and Karol with a K.

"Speak of the devil," said Shawn.

"And he shall appear," said Nathan.

He took a seat beside V again.

"You okay?" she asked.

"Yeah," said Nathan

He gave her a kiss.

"We were just talking about DMT. Have *you* ever heard of it?" Shawn asked.

Nathan cleared his throat and shook his head. "Uh, no. Should I've?"

"Well it's the most powerful, and most natural drug in the world. Dimethyltryptamine is its name, and it's the purist psychedelic you could ever take. AND, it's everywhere."

"How do you mean?" asked Karol.

"It's a compound. You can find it in grass, in the human brain, everywhere. Every single life form has Dimethyltryptamine in it. But one plant in particular, a type of mimosa in Brazil, has root bark that houses a high concentration of DMT. And if you smoke it, it opens your mind, wider than shrooms ever could."

"Imagine the plant's life," said Nathan.

"Well plants aren't alive like us," said V.

"Oh I actually heard that, like, trees can communicate to each other using scents," Karol said with excitement.

"Yeah that's true," added Shawn. "Every living thing is conscious just by being alive."

"And non-living. Just on a bigger scale," Nathan threw in.

"The grand universe," said Karol in a lively voice. Nathan grinned. The group was in a buoyant mood. "Well we won't know until we die."

"You know, I recently heard that ninety percent of your body is made up of bacteria. So ninety percent of you isn't even you," Karol continued.

"And even with that ten percent of you, every five years, you're no longer composed of the original atomic structure that first made you," said Nathan.

After her moment of silence, V hopped back into the conversation. "That's why sometimes in your memories, you feel like a stranger to yourself… because you're no longer that person," Her mind was officially blown.

"That's a sad thought," Shawn threw in.

"Yes and no," said Nathan. "In the end there may be no true self, just scrambled atoms keeping a strange shape together called you, a shape that's always changing; the Theseus' paradox. But the other way of looking at it is that we are all one…" He was feeling a change. The bulk was kicking in. "A collective that *is* the universe. We are all one, we just forget in our waking lives…"

Everything began to vibrate around him until his surrounding were being shaken violently. He sat unmoved by the turbulence, then everything flew down in the blink of an eye. He was greeted with stars, leading him to assume that he made his way into space. A dot in the dark grew in front of him. Closing in at incredible speed, the dot was the planet Jupiter.

"Nathan," the mysterious woman called. Her voice was soft. For the first time it sounded like a whisper *outside* of his head. "If you wish for safety only look within. It was built by those who came after you, and traversed long before they have ever been born…"

Her voice faded out. In Jupiter's orbit the natural satellite Europa closed in, and pulled Nathan down. He passed through a crevasse that spanned down the horizon. Descending at a hazardous speed, he plunged into the dark ocean depths. All was black, and Nathan was alone. He had no sense of his surroundings, and it left him troubled.

"Who are you?" Nathan asked.

A dim glow appeared in front of him. The glowing had a pulse, like a radio signal. Behind the light was a mysterious aquatic creature. It may have resembled an octopus. "I am Synophy, and you must heed me. The darkness is coming. You have little time. It will come from the sky, and set fire to your cities. I know not how it came to be, but *you* will be the only one who can stop the inevitable, and save your world." The light shined bright, then dimmed. In front of the light Nathan could now see himself. "You must prepare."

Nathan looked at his own face in the warm glow, and a slimy slug faded into view, to perfect scale of his body. Following the slug came a blossomed tulip, then a canary, then an old Indian man. Then a chameleon, an ant, and a tree-

Nathan gasped. "It's me."

They were all him; his past lives. They stacked in front of each other with increasing speed, tens to hundreds to thousands, until the light pulsed bright, wiping them all away.

The light pulsed again, like a sonar, showing Nathan other lights. He was now back in the room, looking downward into the core of the Earth. The Earth had a pulse to it, which sounded like a distant thunder storm. He looked up and saw glowing energy sources coming from the people in the room with him. Shawn, V, and Karol were hyper distinguishable from each other. Shawn's energy source had a dim thread connected to Karol as they conversed.

Nathan's eyes slowly opened, wiping away the light show under his eyelids. And just like that, it was gone. "Woah…"

"Nathan!" V exclaimed. "Are you okay?"

"Look who's back," said Shawn. He slapped Nathan's knee. "It's been hours, man. How was the trip?"

Nathan was at a loss for words.

"What happened?" asked V.

"I… don't know," he claimed.

\*

The four companions stood at Shawn's front door and watched as a taxi rolled up to his driveway. Karol hugged Shawn tight.

"It was nice meeting you!" She pulled back and gave Shawn a kiss. "Thanks for having me. Nice meeting you V and Nathan. Bye!"

And with that, Karol skipped away, down the driveway and into the taxi. The three waved as the taxi drove off and down the street.

"Should I have mentioned I was gay?" Shawn asked calmly.

"What?!" shrieked V.

Nathan laughed. He never knew, but he always had a hunch. "It's been good seeing you again Shawn."

"You too man."

Nathan gave him a hug, then V.

"We should head out too," said V. "Let you get some rest."

"Alright… You know, you two may not feel it yet,

but you're both entwined with each other," Shawn used his index fingers to demonstrate. "Like leopard slugs."

Nathan frowned. "That's some reference."

Shawn gave him a nod, as if to say 'I know,' then turned around and walked into his house. Nathan and V walked down his driveway, and away, into the ever warming morning.

"Leopard slugs," Nathan said, mockingly.

V chuckled. "You want to go somewhere for breakfast?" she asked whilst wrapping herself around his arm.

"Yeah," he replied, giving her a kiss on the cheek. "I am fuckin' famished."

"I feel like I haven't eaten in days."

"Last night was fuckin' crazy."

"I've been to Shawn's a ton before, but it seems every time *you* go, something crazy always happens," said V.

"You know, it was the weirdest thing, fighting that guy back in twenty-seventeen."

"How so?" she asked.

"Well I never fought before, first off, and somehow I took him down."

"Maybe you're just a natural. Like one of those people that get into animal modes and see nothing but red."

"It wasn't anything like that. I didn't feel angry, I felt focused. All my pain disappeared, and I looked at him like a test I had been studying for. It almost seemed as if time slowed down too."

"You have a natural talent for fighting," V concluded.

"I don't like fighting."

"Awww." V gave Nathan a kiss.

\*

Nathan and V sat on the jungle gym in their local, vacant park, eating breakfast sandwiches.

"Did you have any, mind-blowing realizations while I was passed out?" asked Nathan.

"Yeah I think I did, kind of..." V said with a nod as she ate.

"What was it?"

"Well... why were we, humans, given contemplative life? Only to die just the same as all animals?"

"It's a little unfair, yeah."

"The human condition; it's... the cruelest, and most beautiful thing, existence has ever conjured up."

Nathan nodded. "Coming from a human."

V nodded sarcastically and they laughed.

"So. The nomad punks. Are they waiting for you somewhere?" he asked.

"Mmn," she answered with a nod, as she finished her sandwich. "Yeah. Depending on how long I'd be, two different cities. They're still in Alberta."

"Oh okay, cool. So how did you get into that? You were going to tell me last night but we got interrupted."

"Yeah yeah. Well, it all started a little while after graduation. My old friends and I went to this one club up north called *The Barn*. I met a guy there, Brad, and we started seeing each other."

"And he was part of the gang?"

V sighed. "Yeah. And so I ended up joining his crew. The first girl to."

"Congratulations. So you married into the family," he said jokingly.

V humphed a grin, but with a sadness behind it. "We ended things a little while after that, but were fine being friends."

"Okay."

"…Then one night at a club, the leader, Skull… uhm, tried to rape me, and…"
She was tearing up. Nathan looked at her with empathy and silence.

"Brad threw him off me, and Skull stabbed him. He disappeared, and no one has seen him since."

"Wow."

"I thought about coming home, but I ended up staying with the gang. They treat me like family, and the lifestyle's all I've ever wanted; to be free."

Nathan stood up and jumped off the jungle gym. He lit a cigarette, and handed it to V. "Let me join," he said with a certainty that glimmered in his strange eyes.

"What?"

"I want to be a part of your family."
V took a pull, and scrutinized Nathan, then gave him back the cigarette. A smile was growing on her face. "What about your job? Your life?"

Nathan waved them away with his hand, and V let out a laugh through her nose.

"Okay. But it's not up to me! We all have to agree."
He hopped up the gym and kissed her. "Okay, whatever it takes," he said as he wiped away one of her tears.

*

# PART II
## Deviance
### (Aberrance)

# Chapter Six:
## ~Initiation~

Nathan looked into his eyes from the rear-view mirror of his Altima. "My dad must have felt like this when he met my mom's family for the first time," he whispered before advancing from his car. The Tuesday morning was windless, sending chills up his spine. He marched on, down the parking lot to the other side where the bike gang sat. They were leaning on their bikes, looking cool. V was alongside them, smirking as Nathan made his appearance. His nervousness spilled over the top of his head, leaving behind an invisible trail of slime.

"Nathan, this is Sal," V said as he entered their circle. She was lightly twisting a large hunting knife on her index finger. The knife was a jungle king, very intimidating. She head-nudged in Sal's direction, and the man waved. He was the owner of that voice from outside the bar over a week ago. He was definitely the oldest of the crew, looked to be in his early forties. He had fair skin and a black pony tail.

"Lookin' a little pale kid," Sal remarked to Nathan's complexion.

"Uh, yeah," Nate said with a huff and a smirk to dismiss the claim.

"Toemat," V continued, pointing with her knife to the shortest man next to the biggest bike. Toemat reminded Nathan of Speedy Gonzales a little bit. "And Greg." The man with the bleach blonde hair. He had a skinny bike. Made him look like an adrenaline junkie. "And, we are the People's Deviants," V said simply.

"...Awesome," Nathan said in response to everyone.

He looked at all their bikes. After the conversation he shared with V at the bar, he decided to do his research. Bikes, bike gangs. The lot. He knew that Sal, for instance, was riding a *Harley Davidson... XR one-twelve X*. Toemat was riding a *Yamaha Bolt Spec five*, and Greg had a *Kawasaki klr*-something or other. V had herself a chunky two-thousand-seven *Suzuki Hayabusa GsX thirteen-hundred R one*.

"You know how to ride?" asked Sal.

"No, but I'm a quick learner."

"Okay. Well, we'll see," he said with a smirk.

*

Nathan stood outside of his boss's office after being truant for two days.

"Step one: quit my job."

Mark was on the phone with a client at the time. "Yeah- I will, I will. Okay, okay, bye. Alright Amon, come on in."

So Nathan did. Mark didn't notice, but Nathan held a certain amount of dread on his face.

"There's the hero! You didn't call in yesterday. And you come in late today..."

"Sorry," he replied. He leaned up against the wall and looked to the ground.

"What's goin' on?"

Nathan took a moment before responding. "Ah, listen I'm sorry but I quit."

"What?"

"I'm not doing the two weeks either. I'm done."

"Hey Amon, come on here I got a schedule to keep, you can't just fucking quit on me. I'm already missing Richard due to his fall!"

He looked at Mark and gave him a tight-lipped shrug. He was trying his best to end his employment as soon as possible.

"Is this about the meteor shit? Our people been talking about how much attention you're giving to those stories. If the top of the world was going to end, moving south won't save you."

Nathan persisted with silence. It made Mark shake his head in defeat.

"Get the fuck out of my office then," he said with woe. His voice also held the stinging sound of disappointment.

Nathan nodded his head, both in understanding and in shame, and walked out of the office. His employment of one year, one month, and seventeen days just came to an end.

Outside of the office, V sat in his car waiting for him.

"How'd it go?" she asked as he made his way up to her.

Nathan made a *not bad* face, dropping the ends of his lips down. "Surprisingly easy."

"Alright. We good to go?"

He got in and buckled up. "Yeah we're good."

"You okay?" she asked.

"Yeah…"

"Sal was right you do not look too good."

"I've just been feeling a little weird after Shawn's. I'm sure I'll be fine."

"It's been two days, but… Alright, if you know you're good." The car roared to life. "Next stop, the bank."

"Yeah," Nathan said with a sigh of relief. He punched his car in drive and rode off, leaving dust in his stead.

*

"Step two: buy a bike."

Nathan's Nissan was parked outside of an automotive dealership. He was inside with V, talking to one of the dealers. The dealer was a tall man with sweaty palms.

"You got a good eye," he said to Nathan. "This is the twenty-fifteen NINJA 300 SE Sport Motorcycle, by Kawasaki. Its features include a four-stroke, liquid-cooled, DOHC, parallel twin engine."

"Fancy," said V, interrupting his spiel.

"Yeah. Now, in its year it was top of the line. It's been six years, so for a sport bike a little outdated, but it rides smoother than some stuff coming out now-a-days."

"Okay," said Nathan with a nod. The look on his face said redundant.

"Its displacement's at two-ninety-six cc, so. You got two-piston hydraulic calipers for your front and rear tires, as well as-"

"I'll take it."

"Ah, you?- Great! Perfect! Okay, follow me and I'll get the paperwork for you."

"I got a question first."

"Yeah?" asked the dealer.

"See my Nissan out front there?"

"Yeah?"

"Well I was thinking of selling it in lieu of the bike. At least, whatever I can make off it."

"Mmm, I don't know. It looks pretty old."

"Yeah, that's what I thought. Okay never mind, paperwork."

"Okay!"

V laughed and wrapped herself around Nathan's arm. The trio made their way into the office.

"Okay. We'll have you fill out these papers here with

your information."

"Yessir."

Name:      Amon Lurani.
Birth Date: 1999 / 04 / 19
Address:    10711 Saskatchewan Dr. Edmonton, AB
Postal:      T6E 4S4

"I don't really have a cellphone."

"That's fine, shouldn't be a problem. How will you be paying today?"

Nathan pulled out a wad of cash.

"Oh! Wow, that uh, that is new."

He began flicking through the bills. "How much is it after taxes?"

"Uhhh. Umh, let's see. It'll come to... four-thousand nine-hundred, sixty-three dollars aaand twelve cents."

Nathan handed him ten bills. "Here's five thousand. Keep the change."

"Okay, great. Thank you so much. And, here are the keys," the dealer said as he swivelled his chair around and picked the keys off the wall.

"I'll take those," said V, reaching out. The dealer handed her the keys and stood up.

"We good to walk this out the front door?" Nathan asked.

"Yeah, by all means."

"Thanks."

"Pleasure doing business with you," the dealer said with an extended hand.

"You too!" Nathan replied. He shook the man's hand, feeling satisfied with his new ride.

*

"Step three: get gear."

The song: *Dreams,* by The Cranberries was playing on overhead speakers. Nathan and V were in sports store, shopping for the essentials: a helmet, a tarp, padding and so on.

"What do you think of this?" He asked her. He wore pads going down his right arm. A shoulder pad, an elbow pad and a forearm pad.

"That's pretty badass."

"Right?... Hey so V,"

"Yeah?"

"I'm starting to feel a bit better now but I got a question I've been mulling over. You ever, think of what dreams are?" he said in reference to the song playing.

"How do you mean?"

"Well like; are they just recycled thoughts, playing in our sleep of the day we just had? Or could they be something more than that?"

"What more could they be?"

"I don't know, like a bridge? Anything, everything. We spend a third of our lives asleep. You think it's just wasted time refreshing our bodies and brains? What if when we sleep we sometimes actually go places? Like parallel worlds. Or our world in the future!"

"Well because it's in the future it's not our world, right? It's another parallel. A possible parallel world that we can reach if we do everything the exact same way as we see it in that dream. But, that's impossible because we always forget, right?"

"What if you remembered?"

"What are you getting at Nathan?"

"I don't know. Nothing I guess."

*

The gang sat around Nathan kitchen table, gorging on his food.

"Okay," Sal began with a full mouth. "We got one simple rule when it comes to stealing: be respectful. That means we typically don't go after family businesses, but if push comes to shove, we will. Corporate establishments are our main target which means security. Security means surveillance. Surveillance means you'll be wanting this."

He pulled out a rolled-up rubber mask of a vampire out of his pocket, and tossed it to Nathan.

"Thanks."

"Don't mention it."

"So, V laughed at this, but I thought buying a pellet gun would be a good idea."

He pulled out a see-through pellet gun with an orange tip at the end of the barrel. Toemat and Greg laughed at Nathan, but Sal just smirked.

"It's not as good as the real thing," Sal said, pulling his shirt up to show Nathan a Grand Power K100 hidden at his waist, "but I think we can do something here."

He stood up, popped the tip off, and walked to the counter. He layered some paper towels down, then whipped out a black spray paint can and sprayed the gun completely until it resembled Sal's. He lit a cigarette then said, "Voila! We'll let this thing dry then head out."

"We can't sleep here?" Greg asked.

"No. Mr. Amon here is registered under this address. He just bought a bike under it, and if anyone sees a bike leaving a crime scene tonight it might lead back here. Better they don't find a bunch of bikes where his car used to sit. Speaking of which, Toemat."

"Yeah."

"Where'd you take that thing?"

"Where you told me."

"We don't want to have to run like last time-"

"I hid it good this time, trust me."

"Alright. Nathan, you ready to do this?"

"Ready or not, I'm all in," he said nervously. The cold sweats were coming back. He tried to conceal it.

"Okay, you'll be fine, just get in and get out as quickly as possible. Don't get distracted."

"Okay."

*

"Step four: rob a store."

Nathan took five minutes just to park his new motorcycle properly. The street was dark and seemingly empty. He began walking down the street to the plaza where an unsuspecting employee was about to get robbed.

"Can I really do this?" he asked himself. He felt woozy.

Time was running out. His life of conformism to the status quo was about to change. The plaza lights shone on his face and he stopped. This was it, Nathan's conversion to the People's Deviants. He snapped the mask on and pulled out his gun, then with a few quick breaths, he marched forward to the Mac's Convenience Store. -ding, ding-

"Give me all your FUCKING MONEY!" Nathan screamed.

Two people ducked behind isles. The worker behind the counter shot his hands in the air.

"Do it, NOW!"

The terrified middle-eastern man opened the till and scooped the cash out of the register. Nathan filled his pockets with the cash and bolted out the store. He sprinted down the street and jumped on his bike. Leaving the mask on, he started up his Ninja and sped away. Street lights blurred passed him. The wind he was creating teared his eyes. His heart was thumping in his ears.

"Holy shit, holy shit, holy shit, holy shit, holy shit," he mumbled nervously to himself as he made his way onto the highway. His initiation was now complete. Nathan pulled the mask off his face and stuffed it in his jacket pocket.

'So that's it. I'm really in. I'm really doing this.'

He turned up highway eight-thirty, heading north. The crew were on the left, in-between five forty and Josephburg. Nathan tried to determine what that would be, but figured he may hit Josephburg and double back.

It was probably around one o'clock. The crisp Wednesday morning country side was lit by an almost full moon as Nathan rode. His heartbeat was slowed now and he could enjoy the feeling.

'I'm going on a journey now.'

Then a flashlight from the side of the road clicked on him. It was V. She was waiting for him, God knew how long. He wobbled his motorcycle around and walked back to her.

"Thanks," he said without a smirk.

"No problem."

She gave him a hug and they walked together into the rough lands before the woods. A dim light grew into a fire the closer they walked and Nathan found himself in the woods with his car again, and the gang.

"How'd you do?" Sal asked, clearly excited as he stood up from his seat. He had a way of smiling on the inside and somehow still being seen. That was the first time Nathan saw it.

Nate reached into his pockets and pulled out fifties,

twenties, and five-dollar bills all crumpled up together.

"They didn't have much cause of loss prevention, but I think I got around four hundred."

"Yeahaha!" Toemat shouted.

"Alright, good one," said Greg.

Sal grinned and patted Nathan on the shoulder. "C'mon 'n grab a seat."

They all took their seats again around the fire.

"We gotta patch your jacket," said Toemat. Nathan gave a confused face and V explained, "Now that you're one of us."

She pointed to the shoulder of her jacket, showing Nathan a sharp-looking *PD* stitched to the leather with lane dividers in the space under the Ps loop. Sal gave Nathan a cigarette and sparked it for him.

"Thanks," Nathan said with a puff.

"So?" V asked.

"How was it? To steal from someone?" Nathan said.

"Yeah," she said with a laugh.

"It was, fuckin'…" he put his palms up and shook his head to say he couldn't say.

"Yeah well get used to it cause that's how we make a living mostly," said Sal. "We also do jobs for people we know sometimes, but our living comes from thievery. You're with us now Nathan."

"You're one of the People's fuckin' Deviants now," Greg concluded.

In the second following, Toemat snapped his finger and pointed hard at Nathan, the act of a man who just remembered something about someone. "…Show me your eyes."

"What?" Nathan asked, bewildered by the question.

"Don't you what me, kid," the short Hispanic man said with a smirk. "The things V's said about you are too crazy to be true. Show me she's lying."

"Toemat what in the fuck," Sal began as Toemat walked over from his seat to stand in front of Nate and bend over with his hands on his knees. Then Sal remembered. "Oh yeahhh! Mister Nathaniel, the man with ocean blue, diamond eyes."

"I don't have diamond eyes," Nathan tried to explain while swatting Toemat away with no success. Toemat just grabbed his head and got even closer.

"Nice try." Silence fell on the gang, until, "I saw it!" Toemat exclaimed. "A lil' shimmer; a tiny dot." He got even closer. "Don't blink so much."

Nathan tried his best to comply but it made him feel terribly awkward.

Time floated, the beers were drunk, and the crew fell asleep. Nathan looked at the fireless pit filled with embers now in a state of reflection. The wind picked up a bit and blew smoke in his face so he waved it away with squinted eyes. But, he noticed something. A few of the embers rolled right and left with his hand. Was it the wind? He looked at them closely, and waved his left hand again. Right, and left; and they moved!

"How is?!… How… Uhgh," he grumbled, before collapsing on the ground.

*

# Chapter Seven:
## ~Fever~

The dark stage of Nathan's mind was ready again to be filled with omnipotence. His body lay unconscious in a deep, cold sweat while his mind was far, far away. He began to hear a noise; a humming. The 'music' sounded like angels remixed by a synthesizer. A red flickering haze came into view, dimly lighting his surroundings. The brighter it got, Nathan realized that the light was not flickering, but he was moving and the light came from the sky only to be blocked by trees. The trees on either side of him kept shooting past until they were all whipped away to reveal a long stretch of highway, disappearing into the horizon. The sky seemed to be laced with a menacing twilight, about to be accompanied by an army of thick storm clouds rolling in.

Nathan looked down to his feet and saw himself standing straight with lane dividers zipping by, no more than an inch under him. The moment he noticed this, his posture changed into the motorcycle seating position. His Ninja appeared under him, and just like that he was off riding alone on the desolate highway.

Lightning began to strike all around him as the storm clouds made their arrival over his head. They set trees aflame and cracked the ground. What was more, the lightning seemed to be coming out of one point in particular. Nathan knew something was above the clouds but could not move to see. He rode on and in the distance a metropolis came into view. Just as this happened, his head cocked up and he saw in the thick clouds awful large tentacles the size of skyscrapers waved about as if they were under water. A mere few seconds after, an outrageously thick bolt of lightning struck the road in front of him. One clean chunk the highway dropped, sending Nathan flying in the air. He landed on the other side of the canyon with a tumble, hitting the ground and rolling. When he got up, a man he'd never seen before was standing right in front of him. He had buzzed blonde hair and a malicious grin like he just got away with murder. His right arm thrusted forward and stabbed Nathan in the abdomen. In a petrified state of shock, Nathan looked down to see his wound and fell backwards into a hole full of water.

He sank down, and found himself surrounded by water as far as the eye could see. Then he started choking. His head felt fuzzy, and just as everything faded away...

Greg nudged Nathan awake.

"Shh. C'mon," he said, then walked off.

Nathan's clothes were drenched in sweat. He caught his breath, then picked himself up and walked over to his bike. The two of them snuck away from everyone else and got onto the road.

"Jesus, you look like death," Greg remarked.

"I actually feel like I almost died," Nathan admitted.

"Alright well come on, You're on me," said Greg before putting on his helmet and speeding off.

Nathan started up his Ninja and went after him. They rode for a while, going north. He still couldn't shake the sweats.

'What's wrong with me?' he thought to himself.

They came to a stop at someone's property. The lot looked pretty run down. It had old, busted up cars littered everywhere.

"What are we doing here?" Nathan asked in a hushed voice.

"You'll see," said Greg. He got off his bike and

walked into the property. Nathan was hesitant but followed along. They made their way around to the backyard. The house was run down, abandoned looking with all the windows boarded up.

"Does anyone live here?"

"I'm gonna guess not," said Greg. "Sal, Toemat and I found this place on Sunday and it gave Sal an idea."

He stopped them at a plain white pickup truck, parked in front of a tall concrete wall. Nathan was feeling better, but still had no idea what they were doing. Greg unzipped his backpack and gave Nathan bolt cutters, then made his way to the driver's side door. Something was definitely going on, like Sal asked Greg to take Nathan with him, and Greg didn't want to. Nathan assured himself it would resolve itself and focused on where he was. He instinctively cut the lock on the tailgate and gave it a pull to see if it would open. It did, showing him nothing but an empty flatbed. He walked over to Greg, who had two flat-blade screwdrivers wedged in the door and a clothes hanger warped into a lock-popper in between them. He was fiddling to unlock the door.

"Anything inside?" he asked.

"Nope. It's empty," said Nathan. Met with silence, he added, "This place is pretty cool."

"Yeah."

"So how long you been a freedom rider?"

"Freedom is as freedom comes, right diamond eyes? It's subjective, like reality." Nathan didn't say anything. Greg changed his tone. "This is my version of being free though. Works for me; I'm happy."

"Alright."

"So you and V," he continued.

"Yeah?"

"You know she was with Brad?"

"Yeah."

"You know Brad was my best friend?"

Nathan frowned at him. "And Skull was Sal's. I'm not an asshole Greg. I love her."

Greg stopped his fiddling. "I'm... sorry." He tried again, and popped it up. With a satisfied look on his face he put his gear away.

"So, what are we doing with this truck?" Nathan asked.

Greg smiled at him and answered, "This'll be your first bank robbery."

\*

The pickup truck was on the road, heading north to the town of Westlock. Everyone was inside with their motorcycles. Sal was driving, with the rest of the gang in the flatbed.

"Okay!" shouted Sal. "The town we're hitting, Westlock, has two corporate credit unions: The Cash Store, and Servus Credit Union. You and V, Greg, got The Cash Store. And you, Toemat, and Nathan got Servus. Hit 'em fast and hit 'em hard, then rendezvous down the road from Husky, up one-oh-four. Nate 'n V, follow Greg and Toemat okay?"

"Kay," "Yeah," said V and Nathan

The truck came to a stop and Sal got out. He ran around to the tailgate, lifted it up, and pulled the ramp out. The gang filed out with their bikes and hit the road. Greg zipped away heading west, with V on his tail. Toemat roared off in the same direction, and Nathan followed. Greg and V got quite a distance ahead of them, but could still be seen. Then Toemat turned right, into a plaza.

"Whew, okay. This is it," Nathan said to himself.

The two rolled passed the building to the back end of the parking lot, around the corner on the right side. They readied themselves; getting off their bikes and prepping their guns. The difference being that Toemat's, like Sal's, was real.

"What're you cocking that for?" Nathan asked.

"What are you twelve? We're robbing a fucking bank store man," said Toemat with utter conviction. He slid his Guy Fawkes mask on and gave Nathan a light shoulder smack. "C'mon."

He proceeded to the building. Nathan hesitated for a moment, baring slight remorse on his face. But he covered it up with the vampire mask... and followed Toemat as he rushed around the corner and into the Servus Credit Union.

"You!" Toemat shouted with his gun raised as they busted into the store. The lady sitting in front of them screamed.

"Give me all your cash, right fucking now."

The store was empty, luckily, so Nathan just stood by and watched. Toemat walked behind the counter and pressed his gun to the lady's temple while she emptied the register.

"The, the police are on their way," she said with a shaky voice. Toemat grabbed the cash from her and stuffed it in his pockets.

"Yeah I figured. Have a nice day."

And with that, the two ran out of the store.

"You were expecting cops?" Nathan asked while they ran to their bikes.

"Yeah of course. If we're lucky the cops'll be after Greg and V."

Just as he said that however, sirens could be heard approaching.

"Fuck! Let's go!" yelled Toemat as he revved his

Bolt. They both took off from the plaza heading east. The siren showed its face as the cop car whipped around the corner behind them. Nathan looked back, his heart pumping like a race horse, and missed Toemat turning left at a street they passed. He looked back in the same second Toemat disappeared down the side street.

"Oh fuck," Nathan spat with clenched teeth. The cop stayed on him, sending him into panic. What was he to do, outride a cop? His mind became a scattered subway system that took to a memory in mind of the current situation. Two, actually. The moments in his life when it was life or death to him. He took a gulp of oxygen, along with other things, and renewed his arborist culture by stating the one tree that made him superman.

"Dawn, Redwood." Redwood… 'Oh…' It did the trick…

Nathan felt the surge in the second. His vision fuzzed before becoming lock solid. His grip on his Ninja clenched, and he swerved left, (north,) down an early morning street. The cop followed suit behind him, but that cop had no idea what he was up against. Nathan swivelled again, right this time. Then left, then right, and left, and left. He actually did it! Though the chase wasn't over yet, Nathan knew he had it. On the edge of the corner street that was coming up, he saw a backyard gate open, and decided to ride straight into the yard, believing he would be safe to hide there.

Next thing he knew he slung off his Ninja and closed the wooden gate behind him. The cruiser roared down the street, past Nathan while he and his Ninja watched behind the fence. The time to relax had finally come… Only the house wasn't empty. Of course it wasn't. A man opened his back-sliding door, letting the news playing on the T.V. project outside as he confronted Nathan.

"Hey what the fuck are you doing?" the man asked

with authority. Nathan's ears tuned in to the T.V. for one second to hear the female news anchor say, "-to the countdown, of the meteo-" and his eyes focused on what the man was doing. He was packing all his belongings. It looked like he had a wife and children that might have already left. The man then charged inside to grab his house phone. "I'm calling the fucking cops."

Without a single word Nathan bolted out of the gate with his Ninja, and the man called out to him. "Yeah run! You fuckin' mistake."

*

A surprising amount of time passed Nathan by as he attempted to find a more suitable area to hide. It must have been close to noon, considering; though it wasn't summer yet, so Nathan couldn't tell from the sun, but he figured he spent enough of two hours walking cautiously with his Ninja.

"Sal and everyone is long gone by now," he said to himself in despondency. Would he never see his love again? He sighed.

Walking down the road it occurred to him that it felt a little too empty. Absolutely *no one* was outside. Vacant streets in the middle of the day let him know just how serious the meteorite warning was to the people of Westlock.

The second he saw a bike trail appear through the suburbia, it excited him. Nathan made his way across the street to the ravine and entered with caution. You never know what kind of cult-like behaviours might go down in a small town of upper Alberta. Luckily Nathan found himself alone. He rested his bike down and covered it with a blue tarp he bought on his shopping spree. A stump near the bike caught his eye and he took a seat.

Nathan gazed upon the nature in front of him, and a thought he once had struck him. "Oh!"

He flipped the tarp up and scrounged through his Ninja sac and pulled out his notebook and a pen.

-21/04/28-

'Dear Journal,

Times have very much changed. V is again in my life and I am willing to do anything to keep her close. My occupation was the first sacrifice. The next was my apartment, and my sense of security. Last Saturday her and I ate shrooms for the first time. My dreams have been strange since late June of my graduation, and now I might have an idea as of why. The older woman is no woman, but a creature. I still have no idea about my ghost sister, but like all things I believe that time will tell. No longer should I think of my dreams as strange. They may just verge on prophetic. If they truly somehow are, then a terrible fate lies on this world... and what? Am I really supposed to stop it? How? I won't give up on my sanity so easily. On that I remain heavily sceptical.

On another note I also had dream last night. I was riding down a highway alone and there was something in the sky. I don't know what, but now not to jump to conclusions, but something also happened last night right before I passed out. I think I might actually have moved something... without touching it. Actually I'm certain I did.

Precognition. Telekinetic, fucking, manipulation... With no time I've actually had to ponder the possible theories that could explain everything that's been happening to me, all that I can think of now is that it has something to do with the shrooms? But there's more to it than that. People don't just gain super powers from doing drugs. The back of my head is still tingling a little. I don't know if that has to do with the sweats I've been having or not, but- oh yeah! The word- which I'll now use in extreme caution: DAWN REDWOOD, allows me to perceive everything at a higher rate. Like a Kung Fu master or something. I'll try to watch that… but seriously. To transcend the physical bounds of my body is… super, powers. I mean just to think of the things I could potentially do! I could use these powers, tread paths of glory for others to follow in.'

Nathan huffed at himself. "Jesus."

He pulled out a cigarette from his jacket pocket and lit it. He exhaled the smoke, and began to feel dizzy. The sweats came back with it. His breathing got heavy.

"Oh no."

His vision blurred, and right before everything went black, the leaves around him shuffled and twirled like a twister. Then, -THUD-.

-BZZZ-

-VVVY-

-AHHH-

-WHHH-

Buzzy, beady, blurry blackness. Cold and hot and wet and dry. High, and light. Then down and ground. Nathan came to… and felt a sense of fatigue lift from him as the stability of his motor functions returned. His notebook and pen lay in the leaves and twigs. His Ninja was still intact, still hidden. He breathed a sigh of relief. But hours had passed. No memory of a dream this time, and he felt like he just survived a heart attack.

"What the fuck is happening to me," he mumbled.

He groaned as he lifted himself up. Clarity clasped his conscience again. The colours came with it. He grabbed his notebook and pen again, and stashed them away in his

Ninja. He took a seat once more on the stump and sat with the sun, which was resting on the horizon. Then it came to him. The ember, the leaves, the foreboding aquatic Europian. He actually did have something here. He thought back to the film: *Scanners*, and how unique individuals used their minds to move objects. They would focus where they wanted something-!

Nathan swept his left hand across the ground, and leaves brushed in the same direction. Not like wind did it, but like someone actually scraped the ground with their hand. He felt a tingling sensation again, like what he felt when he evaded the police cruiser. It started in the back of his head, then flushed down his spine. This was it. But what was it? Nathan tried again but this time he lifted his arm and focused on a fallen branch in particular. A vibrating noise filled the inside of his head. He flexed, and the stick began to elevate off the ground. Only by inches, but inches none the less. With absolutely zero physical contact, Nathan was moving solid objects. He aimed his power at a larger branch on the ground, a limb, and hoisted it up. It wobbled the higher he rose it, but it stayed suspended. With his left arm he kept it up, and with his right he gave a swing with a closed fist. The limb shattered in half, shocking Nathan into releasing his grip, and the two halves to drop on the ground.

"Oh my God."

*

# Chapter Eight:
## ~Let's Fight~

"NATHAN?!" Nathan heard V scream from the road far above.

'Holy shit did she see that?!'

"Diamond eyes!" Sal yelled.

The two of them ran down to him, in a manner that assured him they were not present for his event, and Sal hugged him hard, hoisting him off the ground. "Jesus fuck man!" he yelled.

Nathan got his footing again, and looked to V who was overwhelmed with relief.

"Thank God you made it," she breathed.

"Toemat said you got a pig on your tail," Sal continued.

"Haha yeah I got away, no thanks to Toemat!" Nathan yelled to the air.

"Hey," Toemat's voice echoed from the highlands.

"You won't believe how much money Greg and I got!" V exclaimed.

"What are we talking?" asked Nathan feeling eager for her.

"Almost ten grand!!"

"WHAT?!" Nathan burst. He was happy for the People's Deviants, of course, but his excitement was also for his own little secret, that he was now expressing through their earnings.

"C'mon," said Sal. "You and me are ditching the truck."

"Okay," said Nathan. The three made their way up the ravine. V got in a car with Tomat and the accomplice driver, and Nathan rolled his Ninja into the back of the pickup truck. The car went off and Nathan hopped into the pickup with Sal, and they were off.

They hit the road with Nathan's bike rattling in the flatbed.

"So! What's the story behind you and V?" asked Sal. "I think it's high time I found that out."

"She didn't tell you?"

"No."

"Well," Nathan began. "We've been classmates since grade five. We never really talked though. As a kid I was really shy."

"Well you sure as fuck aren't now hahaha!" said Sal. He pat Nathan on the chest.

"Yeah I don't know, life changes you. It definitely started thanks to V. I never had much motivation growing up."

"Yeah."

"Then everything changed on graduation. She was working at the Timmy's right near my house-"

"And that was your motivation?"

"Yeah hahaha, to talk to her."

"Yeah yeah."

"Eventually I did, but then uh, my dad died. And I ran away."

Silence sat for a moment. "Well fuck man, how would anyone react."

"Yeah. Uh, I came to terms with it in time, but by then it was too late you know? She was gone, and I was living in Alberta. A bit out of the way."

"Yeah," Sal said in a light-hearted tone.

"So I kept on, just doin' what I was doin'. But there wasn't a moment that I didn't regret leaving her."

"Well you guys are back together now right? Kinda

like it was meant to be or something."

"You could say that… Yeah, that's what I'd like to believe."

Sal smiled. "You know I was in love once."

"Oh yeah?"

"Yeah…" Sal looked forward at nothing. His body drove, but he was somewhere else. "There's one thing I'll always miss: going on dinner dates. There was just something about it, I don't know."

"I've never been on one."

"No? You're missing out."

Sal stole another moment of silence before saying, "We're not meant to be alone in this world, Nathan. That's what *I'd* like to believe."

\*

Nathan and V danced together in a crowded, sweaty club with the gang somewhere in the room. Sal's conversation echoed in Nathan's head as the two jumped to the music, which was a house version of *Kangaroo Court* by Capital Cities. Sweat dripped, lights swam, and people flowed. The majority of which were on an excess of drugs. Mostly MDMA, but also many alterations of it. The behavioural additives moulded and morphed the dance floor with clay tectonic and liquefiers. Nathan and V found themselves in a sea of mind-altered partiers, and could not care less.

"You know I love you," V whispered in his ear and the two began wildly making out.

Nathan couldn't hold his sexual urges back any longer. He grabbed V's hand and took her out of the club. The two ran out from the building and into the close-by woods. They ventured farther and farther, until they came across a crop of motorcycles, hidden from the public.

Nathan lay V down on the soft, dirty ground and began making out with her again, but more passionately. Bliss and ecstasy released in his mind as he moved his hands down her body, refamiliarizing himself with her curves. The leaves made ruffling noises under her. It was all that could be heard aside from their moaning, and the trees bending to the slight nighttime breeze. She rubbed her hands down his chest, feeling his muscles. She didn't realize until now how much more muscular he'd become. Nathan's hand reached V's pants, and he began rubbing her crotch. She let out a loud moan through their snogging, and grabbed at Nathan's penis. In seconds they had each other's pants down, and for the second time in each others' lives, they made love.

*

"I am the master of pulling out!" Toemat declared to Greg.

Nathan almost spilled his beer on himself mid-sip. "What are they talking' about?" he asked Sal with a chuckle.

"I don't know. And he is not the master, I'll tell yah somethin'…"

V laughed a giddy laugh. The three of them sat together at a round table watching Greg and Toemat play darts.

"Okay you ready?" V asked Nate.

"Yeah," said Nathan, and the two kicked back a shot. They both winced. "Mnn. Nope, nope."

"Okay this is the last one, ready?"

"Yeah," and they kick another back.

V's face scrunched up.

"That was it! Ginger blood is a prairie fire!"

"Oh my God that was terrible," said V.

Sal patted Nathan on his shoulder as he sat up. "I'll be right back."

Nathan looked up and watched Sal approach the bar near two men who were having a 'discussion'. One of them looking a little more than tipsy.

"Hey V," said Nathan, pointing to Sal.

"Another Canadian, please," Sal asked.

"Sure thing," said the big bartender who looked to be in his late twenties. He popped off the top and handed Sal the bottle. "Hey, I wasn't going to say anything before," the man began which put a look of readiness on Sal's face, "but, isn't your name like Salvador or something like that?"

"Or something like that. Who's asking?"

The bartender waved his hand with a shake of his head to take the tension out of the conversation. "My old man used to work the pub in Rosthern, north of Saskatoon. He'd keep me after class in high school to teach me character."

"I'll be damned, you're Jim's kid."

The bartender smirked. "Yeah, yeah that's right. I remember your gang. You and that one guy Skull."

"Yeah, well, we don't roll anymore."

"I heard. I also heard something recently. You don't have to believe me, considering I'm a stranger and all, but I got word he's back, and he's in the G.T.A."

"Who? Who told you that?"

"No one. I overheard it a few times over Christmas break when I was in the area. Hell of a thing I ran into you all the way out here."

"…Yeah. Yeah that's a hell of a thing," Sal said as he looked at nothing in particular with a frown.

"Hey man listen," the drunk bar patron said to the other quite loudly almost in Sal's ear, shaking him out of his head. "I know I still owe you, but look, I'll have the money by tomorrow I swear."

"That's what you said last night y'piece of shit."

At this point a bald, bearded man from presumably their table, near the front entrance of the bar got up and left to have a cigarette. It left two more people sitting and watching the show along with Nathan and V at their table.

"Okay well thanks for the information kid, it means a lot," Sal said to the bartender as he prepared to leave back to his table.

"Hey man," the drunkard said with a hushed voice to Sal. "You got a-"

"He's not giving you a goddamned cent."

"You guys!" the drunk now pleaded to the table. "Ricky, Chris, c'mon! The fuckin' world's ending anyway!"

"This ain't gonna become a problem, is it?" Sal asked in the party's general direction.

"It's none of your goddamned business if-"

"Hey! You leave him alone Carl."

"What the fuck's it to you?!"

"You leave him alone," the drunk said with a shove at Carl. Chris got up, feeling heated, and walked to the bathroom. On his way he passed the dart board, where Greg was whacking Toemat with a pool cue.

"You're getting on my last fucking nerves Ron," Carl said as he shoved drunk Ron hard, making him bump into Sal. At this point Nathan and V stood up. Everyone froze. Ron looked at Sal and pointed his finger.

"Heh heh, how 'bout this! We arm wrestle."

"What?" asked Sal, utterly confused.

"And if I win, you give Carl here what I owe."

"Do it," Toemat called out to be a shit disturber, and Sal sighed. Ron, now excited about his chances of paying off his debt walked over to an empty table, in-between the pool table and the dart board. Sal followed along with Carl. Nathan and V took their seats again and watched. The whole bar was watching now at this point. They set themselves up, left palms down to the elbow and everything. Greg stood over them, along with Toemat and Carl, and announced the match.

"Okay! The rules are simple, no cheating. If Ron here wins, Sal pays whatever amount to Carl. If Sal wins… what, Sal."

"Then no one's fighting here. You take it home and deal with it there."

Greg looked disappointed that Sal decided to act so noble. "Okay get ready! Three! Two! One!! GO!!!"

Sal slammed Ron's arm down in the same second the match began. Ron got up and walked to the bar with haste, not looking at anybody, and ordered a pint. The crowd was speechless. Then to everyone's surprise, the bartender gave him the pint.

"And another for Ricky!"

Ricky sat alone at the table awkwardly looking at everyone else, who were all still in a state of disbelief. The one friend who left didn't seem to be coming back, and Chris just now came out of the bathroom, sniffing, like he just got a cold.

Ron looked at Nathan and hollered, "HEY, that's a nice jacket you got there, I want it."

Nathan stood up, staring at the redneck piece of shit, and clenched his fists.

"You got some fuckin' nerve," he said.

V stood up and held Nathan fist. "He's not worth it. C'mon."

Sal, Carl, Toemat and Greg were still standing by the dart board, not doing anything.

"What the fuck's going on," Toemat whispered to Greg.

Then at the other side of the pool table, Chris screamed, disturbed by the silence and high on cocaine, and punched a random man in the face. The bar exploded like a fuse waiting to light. Ron raised his pint glass to Ricky then threw it at Carl. It missed and hit a bystander. The bystander screamed and threw a punch at Sal, landing a hard hit in the jaw.

"Jesus!" V screamed.

Carl and Greg ran at Ron and started punching him, which forced Ricky to get up. He threw Greg off and the two of them started fighting. Sal got the bystander in a sleeper hold and put him down. Then the bystander's friend ran at Sal.

"Oh, come on!"

Tocmat started rummaging the unconscious bystander's pockets, looking up to see if anyone was noticing. Sal grabbed the bystander's friend by one arm, hoisted him off the ground, and threw him against the wall. He hit the ground and lay there, holding himself in pain.

Ricky out of fighters' instinct beat Greg down and was helping Ron beat Carl. Toemat ran to Greg and pulled him out of the fight scene. Chris, now done beating the poor stranger, leaped over the pool table and ran at Carl. Nathan and V finally decided that enough was enough and threw themselves into the fight, to help the man who only wanted his money. Nathan went after cocaine Chris, and V went after Ricky, knowing he didn't want to be there.

Ron noticed that the match had become a little too even and decided to throw Carl off him and help Chris attack Nathan. When Ron shoved Carl, Carl accidentally tripped on the unconscious bystander and knocked his head hard on the ground. V, realizing Ricky had decided to not give up, threw herself over the bar and started throwing bottles at him. He ran out of the bar in a panic, and V started throwing bottles at Ron. The bartender grabbed V and restrained her. He watched on in terror as the bar got destroyed.

Sal ran at the cluster and ripped cocaine-Chris off Nathan, feeding him several shots in the face before he collapsed. Greg got himself up, still feeling weak but ready, and helped get Nathan out of the fight with Ron. Greg and Ron were now at it. Then, the bald, bearded man from before the fight entered the bar again, with Ricky behind him. The man punched Ron hard in the face and dropped him. Then grabbed one of the bottles on the ground and smashed it over Greg's head, finishing the fight. V elbowed the bartender in the gonads and hopped over the bar. Sal and Toemat grabbed Greg and hurried out the backdoor with Nathan and V on their tail.

They ran out into the farmlands until they couldn't be seen anymore, and crouched in the field. Toemat let out a laugh and Sal shushed him. They waited until the ruckus from the bar simmered down to silence.

"Okay, I think we're good," Sal whispered.

Greg groaned. "Oww."

"Hey buddy," Toemat said in a cheerful tone.

V couldn't help herself but snicker.

"...Skull's back in the G.T.A.," Sal addressed to the gang. Everyone's giddiness halted and a sober mood rested between them all.

"Did I just hear that Skull's back?" Greg asked lazily. His voice had a strong undertone of hatred. No one else spoke, and they all just sat there in the tall grass.

*

# Chapter Nine:
## ~The Road~

Crunchy ash vault salted the gas station where the gang was filling their bikes up. Nathan was leaned against his Ninja with his notebook in hand, watching a jeep roll up. A crop of young adults hopped out. The driver began filling up. Two girls got out and walked to the station, and two other guys walked maybe a foot away and lit cigarettes. Greg burst into a speed-walk at the two guys with the potential of making a scene. Toemat followed him and Nathan, with Sal and V, stayed back and watched.

"Hey. Hey!" Greg addressed as he closed in. He got uncomfortably close to the guys, with Toemat on his back.

"You wanna kill us?"

"Woah dude back the fuck off," one of them said looking intimidated.

Nathan tuned them out and got back to his notebook.

-21/04/30-

'Dear Journal,

I've thought of a name for my ability. It will be called: Telekinetic Vibrational Manipulation; the acronym for which is T.V.M. My party of nomad punks continue to travel east and to the south, though in my heart I ache to go northwest and I don't know why. However, my heart can ache all it likes because no matter how much I want anything else, V will come first, even before myself. A few weeks ago word came from my old region saying Skull the flied murderer and attempter rapist is now back. I've never met the man but just through stories I know that he may be the first man I truly hate. No one has talked about it since Sal brought it up but I know we are all thinking about it.

I'm additionally thinking about my powers that I use in secret, and my dreams that scream urgency at me. The People's Deviants are my family now, and I'm in love. How could I possibly give up this freedom?'

He sighed, understanding how his reasons for ignoring a potentially universal shift of the planet's stability was entirely selfish. "Damn it."

*

Weeks on the road turned into months. Nathan fell into place as a brother among the gang, and every day was treated as new and unknown as the last. They travelled east, making new friends along the way. Some nights they would find a bed, some nights they slept outside. On *paydays* if they couldn't find a place, they would treat themselves and buy a room for the night. Every year the gang rode across the country, left and right, passing through new towns each time. They stayed relatively crime free in the major cities and made connections instead. When the winter time came, they bunkered down as best they could with acquaintances.

Although Nathan was still a new member, this lifestyle was nothing new to him; the life of a rubber tramp. In the years after his disappearance, Nathan did his best to get a job and find a place to live. Not in that order, but that was the order it came in. He started out homeless, then began to find a way around staying in one place and sleeping on the streets. He made friends at each new town he found, either through work or otherwise, that helped him with shelter, and before he knew it he had enough money to buy a van. From that point on he became a rubber tramp, working new jobs to make a living then moving on to the next place. When his van died he was stuck in a chilly situation. It was winter, and no one was hiring. The streets were empty, like his wallet and his stomach.

Through perseverance, and the sheer will to live, Nathan survived the cold of winter. Once spring came, he gave in to society again. He could no longer pull off the tramp lifestyle. Situated in Edmonton, Nathan found himself a job and saved up a lump of money before getting himself an apartment. Under the alias of Amon Lurani, he had begun a new life for himself. And then, just as quickly as he had it, V came back into his life, and he was back on the road. A place where he belonged. As a traveller, a doer, not a dreamer like how he spent his youth.

Warm winds blew the trees on the outskirts of Winnipeg. Nathan was outside of a tavern, smoking a cigarette. The door opened and Sal came out to join him.

"Hey Nate, how you doin'?" Sal asked.

"Good man, good. Just can't get over how crazy people are acting the more south we go. It's turning into a pandemic. Makes me wonder how serious this thing really is."

Sal sat a cigarette on his lip and scrummaged through his jacket pockets, looking for a lighter. "Eh, the roads have always been full of crazy people. Only new thing is the fuel on T.V. People have an excuse now to panic; to overreact." Nathan gave his hand and lit Sal's cig for him.

"Thanks," said Sal as he exhaled. "So, uh… you and V talk about," he ruffled his hair, "the future, at all?"

"How do you mean?" asked Nathan.

"You know like, the future of you two. You're both in love. You shouldn't be in a bike gang. People in bike gangs either end up behind bars or dead. I'm a fuckin' marathon runner, I'm no role model… You know there use to be twelve of us, in the People's Deviants? Now there's five. I'm the only one left from the beginning… Just talk to her about it, okay?"

"Okay, I will," said Nathan.

"Alright!" said Sal, rubbing Nathan's head.

"So, I got a weird question Sal but, since the gang started it's never really been about being a motorcycle gang, right? Why motorcycles? Why not like a hippie van?"

"What are you talkin' about?" Sal asked for clarification.

"I mean like you want to live on the road, a motorhome would be a lot better on gas between everyone."

"Yeah probably but it's not about that. It's about each of us on our own, but together, like a herd. Each one has their own preference on what they ride. A motorcycle is just the smallest thing you can use to get around. If I could fly in lieu of a motorcycle I would. The least amount as possible is the best in my opinion."

"So why not a leather tramp?" Nathan asked.

"Leather tramps are doomed to die. On a bike you can get away from a situation fast, you don't have to rely on getting picked up, and you still get to enjoy the land… Leather tramp if I could fly."

\*

Another night and Nate and V had their backs against a gas station wall. The night was dark and the lot was empty. Both of them were masked. Nathan held his air gun, and V had her Jungle King hunting knife.

"You ready?" she asked. Nathan nodded. He took Sal's words of wisdom into consideration. They were about to perform yet another armed robbery, a crime that would put them both away for years. If need be he was confident he could break out, and break V out, but it wasn't worth it to potentially not have what it takes. He needed V in his life. Powers aside, she was the only thing on his mind. His great love.

"Okay, go," she said.

The two bolted into the station with their weapons at the ready.

The following day found the gang stuck in the worst traffic any of them had ever seen. Horns were honking, people were yelling, and overall the atmosphere was one of static desperation. The roads of mid Canada were vastly different from the more populated roads of southern Canada, same as the how north Canadian roads were next to non- existent. As the People's Deviants continued down the main highway and its respective side roads, they entered into the real state of panic the populace was having. Entire towns were being evacuated to bigger cities while most families decided on their own to pass the Canadian/States boarder in hopes of better protecting their loved ones. Nathan absorbed it all as he continued his internal struggle to not act on the matter.

"Turn here!" Sal yelled and the group followed him off the highway. They entered suburban streets and happened upon a subway. The team parked their bikes behind the plaza after ordering subs where Greg would finally vent. "I honestly hate traffic so fuckin' much."

"Well the way I see it is now we stop taking the highway. It'll give us a chance to see more of the beautiful country we live in."

Whilst the gang was wasting time eating lunch by old railroad tracks at the back of the plaza, Nathan conjured up some poetry. Thanks to Sal, he was thinking a lot about what his actual future might be. He knew he was procrastinating. Extra sensory perception and manipulation were real, he knew that now first hand, but he was keeping it a secret from the gang. The reasoning was mostly fear of what it might do to the group. V was happy, and so was he. He didn't want to ruin that. With so much weighing his mind, he put his pen to paper.

-21/06/02-

'And how was I supposed to feel? That's the first thing that popped into my head after writing the date. What would I even do? Go to the nearest government building and say, excuse me but I have the ability to hover logs, may I be of assistance to you on the matter of the meteorites? It's stupid. Stupid and impossible. I can't even muster the courage to tell the gang. Somehow in a way I miss the old days of my adult life. Back then I would have written this:

Dear the coming summer, please bring me peace. Shine on me joy. Something of my childhood, when everything was so big, and new, and endless. I can remember the feeling, but I can't FEEL it anymore. Winters have made me bitter and lame; a cruel indignation. A four-year death season, now coming to a close. Come the summer, and I will be a blossoming tulip to the nuance of festivities. I wait for the day now, when it all comes back to me.'

"You thinkin' at all about how maybe goin' in the direction we're goin' might be a bad idea?" Toemat asked Sal as the two ate alone at the cluster of parked bikes.

"We're going to Caz and the boys in the city, and continuing east to Pattie and her farm, like we always do."

"…I don't ever want a situation like what happened before. I don't want Nathan to get killed trying to defend

V!" Toemat kept his voice down but his words had power.

"That shit's never gonna happen again," Sal said with a clenched jaw. "We'll expect him. And V knows how to defend herself now."

Greg walked over to Sal and Toemat after finishing the creation of a lump of sticks on the railroad tracks. "What are you guys talking about?" he asked.

A second of silence held in the air before Sal said something. "What do you think of Nathan?"

Greg looked over to him as he pocketed his journal and headed over to V who was spray-painting the back plaza wall. "He's a good kid," Greg said with a shrug. "Got a lot of heart. I'm honestly surprised he's cool with all the shit we do."

"Well you know what happened to him," Toemat rhetorically asked.

"Yeah."

"So, his entire family is dead, and yet... He's in love. That's his motivation. Must be for everything," Sal added.

"Yeah maybe," said Greg. "You ever try holding a conversation with him when he gets drunk? It's fuckin' annoying. The guy thinks he's a modern-day philosopher."

Nathan and V were playing around with her spray paint can.

"Ooo," said Nathan as V laced a large *V* on the wall. "Real original."

She shoved him with a smirk on her face. "Fucker. What do you got?"

"Let's see..."

He grabbed the spray paint and began constructing over her work. He turned the *V* into a roman five, and added an N above it.

"N, V; Envy... Awww," she said, with no resistance

in kissing him. "But baby why make the V a five?"

"Well we met in grade five, didn't we?"

She hugged him hard for saying that.

\*

Nathan and Toemat were around the corner of a gas station in Atikokan. They barged the place with guns raised. The cashier had his head down at his mobile phone, watching a funny video before they burst in. Nathan dropped a duffle bag on the countertop. The cashier looked up to Nathan pointing the gun at his face.

"That's an air soft pistol," the cashier said, not amused. Toemat raised his gun and fired it into the ceiling. Nathan and the cashier jumped.

Toemat pointed the gun at the man. "Is this?"

The cashier frantically opened the till and filled the bag, and the two scurried out.

The following night the gang was around a fire in the woods, eating beans.

"What would you call us, diamond eyes?" Toemat asked Nathan.

"…In simple terms we're a bike gang. But we don't hold a territory, or sell guns or drugs, so I think we're *nomad punks.* The name works better."

"Nomad punks?" Sal repeated, impressed.

"Yeah, V thought of it."

"Not bad. Nomad punks. The People's Deviants! Nomad punks!" Greg declared with pride.

In all the time they'd been riding together and pulling off stunts, Nathan still hadn't cracked Greg's surface. He wondered why. He was close with everyone else. It almost reminded him of the relationship he had with his older brother, Alex. Once Alex hit puberty he went off to high school, and became someone else. Having fun became *gay* and they didn't connect anymore.

Greg clearly had a tough exterior because of something that happened to him, but what? It couldn't just be Brad dying, there was something deeper. Nathan wasn't going to jump to conclusions. He took a pull from his dying cigarette and tossed it in the fire.

\*

Situated at another bar, Sal was conversing with a man he met only ten minutes ago.

"So is it cool if we stay the night? And tomorrow we'll get that done for you?" asked Sal.

"Yeah man totally, mi casa es su casa. Thanks again."

Nathan and Greg were sitting together at the time, both watching Sal perform his magic.

"Sal's really good at finding people who need help," Nathan said to Greg.

"Yeah well before he joined the gang he used to be like a social worker or something. Then this one lady he was trying to help stabbed him a bunch of times. Skull pulled the bitch off and killed her. Skull convinced him that the two should hit the road and they did. The rest is history."

"Oh. Wow, that's one hell of a story."

"Yeah."

"What about you?" Nathan asked, testing the waters.

"What, what's my story?"

"Yeah, well how you got in the gang."

Greg shrugged. As he began to speak it was evident in his body language that he was slightly uncomfortable. "I went to college for my parents' sake but fuckin' hated it. I disappeared; got picked up by Brad a week later."

Nathan nodded. "Okay." He knew not to push further.

Coincidentally just as their conversation died, a ruckus erupted from the other side of the bar. A tall man with broad shoulders was holding Toemat by his jacket.

"This mother fucker was picking through my shit while I was in the bathroom!" he said with a glare at the bartender. The bartender raised his hands as to say, 'don't look at me.' Greg and Nathan were on the case. He knew the man was right, but Toemat was their brother.

"I think you were mistaken," said Greg. "Maybe you should let him go."

He looked at Greg and Nathan, contemplating his next move.

"You should fuckin' let me go," Toemat said nervously.

"Shut the fuck up, faggot!"

"Hey! Don't call my friend a faggot!" Greg shouted.

"What's it to you, queer? He your butt buddy?"

That was the trigger. Greg punched the man in the gut, making him release Toemat, who quickly backed away. The man slammed Greg's head into the bar. He crumpled to the ground, holding his head. Nathan flared up. He punched the man in the face as hard as he could, but didn't get much of an affect. The man rolled his shoulders back, releasing loud crack noises. Fear filled Nathan, looking up at the now angered man.

"Dawww... fuck it," said Nathan. He prepared himself for a pummelling, when Sal's fist stretched out and punched the man, staggering him. Nathan didn't think twice; he grabbed Greg and dragged him out. Toemat leaped over and helped him. Sal got picked up and thrown onto a table, collapsing it.

"C'man!!" Toemat yelled to their new friend, who was stuck in shock that a fight just broke out. They got out the door, and Greg found his footing.

"Hey what happened?!" V asked. She was outside having a cigarette, and was... pretty, surprised to see Greg getting dragged out all bloodied up.

"Toemat happened," said Nathan.

"Hey." said Toemat, as was his usual response when he knew he was at fault.

Nathan sighed. "I'm going back in for Sal."

"No Nathan," V pleaded.

He opened the door and looked back to her. "It'll be fine-"

And Sal burst out of the door.

"Let's fuckin' Go!!!" he screamed.

They all got on their bikes; the stranger on Toemat's, and they were off. Out on the road. The roads whipped and spun as they roared away in the night. It began to rain, and Nathan looked back. Behind him was Greg at the end of the line. He seemed to be struggling with his stability. They took a tight turn, and unfortunately to a lack of Nathan's surprise, Greg slipped off his *klr* and slid off the road and into the trees.

Nathan hit the brakes and screamed, "WAIT!" but to no affect. His Ninja skirted to a stop and he walked it to the side of the road, then ran to Greg.

Greg was lying off the road in a cluster of trees, just lying there. His face held remorse, and his body was exhausted. Nathan made his way over to him and gave him a hand. He gave Nathan a pissed-off look that resembled a defeated man being laughed at, and refused his help. Nathan watched as Greg hoisted himself up, clearly in pain.

"Hey man, just let me help you," Nathan impeded, but to no avail.

"I fuckin' got it!" shouted Greg, right before he slumped back down against a tree.

"Hey!!" Nathan shouted at him. "I've had enough of your shit. What the fuck did I do to you Greg?... I know, alright. I know why you got that attitude."

"What the fuck do you know?"

"I know you're afraid. So am I. I've been afraid my whole life. But that doesn't mean you should push people away. We all go through the same things, one way or another."

Nathan gave Greg something to sit on. The rain poured, and after a moment of silence, Greg hauled himself up.

"Brad and I, in the beginning; w-we had a moment."

Nathan thought abut saying, 'I know,' but thought better and stayed silent. Instead he grabbed Greg and hugged him.

\*

The gang were in their new friend's apartment. Nathan and V waited at the bathroom door for Sal to get out of the shower. He exited, nude, rubbing his hair with a bath towel. Nate and V rushed into the shower together. They helped each other undress while kissing and giggling under their breaths. Nathan turned the shower on and tested the heat with his fingers while V rubbed him stiff. They only had the chance to have shower sex once before so there was no way they were going to let the opportunity go by. The apartment dwelling was small, so the gang had to sleep together on the floor like a pack of wolves. Everyone fell asleep, and Nathan lay in the huddle with his eyes open.

'Should I tell them?' he thought to himself. He

looked around the living room for something to manipulate with T.V.M. A beer bottle sat on a cabinet. He focused on it, and lifted it up. More so, he imagined warping the shape of the glass in the middle out of mild curiosity. Nothing happened. He thought about pushing his mental strength a little more but feared the bottle would just break. It hovered over to him and he lowered it onto his forehead. Then he let out a sigh and closed his eyes. The bottle sat angled on his forehead but did not slide. He had a firm invisible grip on it, unlike the tree limb it did not wobble.

"Nathan…" Toemat's shaking voice whispered.

Nathan's eyes burst open. 'Fuck!' he internally screamed. "…Don't move," he decided to say. How he was going to explain himself though he had no idea.

The beer bottle hovered off his forehead and landed smoothly back on the living room cabinet. Everyone else was still asleep. All was silent, and Nathan decided to keep it that way. He just didn't say anything, hoping Toemat would do the same. Hours passed until his eyes finally shut.

The next morning Sal, Greg and Nathan rode to a stranger's house to answer their new friend's request. He had his car stolen from him by one of his sister's ex-boyfriends, and he wanted it back. Sal knocked on the front door and waited for an answer. A man opened the door.

"Hello?" he asked.

"Are you Terry?" asked Sal.

"Yeah," he said, confused.

Sal grabbed him by the collar and shoved him inside. Terry fell backwards and landed on his ass. Greg and Nathan followed Sal inside.

"Where are the fuckin' keys?" Sal demanded. Terry reached up to the stand at the shoe mat and grabbed a car key. Sal swiped it from his hands then added politely,

"Thank you," with a bow.

The three walked out, and Greg n' Nathan helped Sal mount his XR one-twelve X onto the back of the pickup truck.

"Well that was easy," Greg said to Nathan.

More days passed, and the gang tried once again to take the highway. As they sat in more congested traffic a group of ladies on two wheels roared past in the opposite direction. No one was going north but them. Upon seeing them, Sal at the front of the line directed everyone to take a left at some mining site that was luckily just coming up. They all followed in a line and turned around to re-enter the highway on the other side. Nathan was the only one who didn't know what was going on.

They met up with the group off of the thirty-five highway in Azilda, in Ontario, parking near the Doghouse sports bar where the ladies were, but the bar was closed. The People's Deviants walked up to meet the group of ladies.

"Who are we meeting?" Nathan whispered to V as they made their approach.

"These are the Motor Maids, another bike gang. Sal's got a history with one of them."

"Ohh-" said Nate before Toemat grabbed his arm to halt his steps. V looked back and Toemat motioned with his head for her to keep going, so she did.

"Listen Nathan you gotta talk to me man. It's been fuckin' days since that night and you haven't said a word to me about it."

"Well I didn't exactly want to bring it up with everyone around."

"I get that but I can't keep waiting for a chance for us to be alone!" Toemat sighed before continuing. "What was that?"

"What do you think that was?"

Meanwhile the Motor Maids were talking with Sal, V, and Greg. "There are less people the more north we go."

"We could have told you that. Entire towns are deserted," said Sal.

"It looks like this one is too," one of the females remarked.

"Every city will still have some people in them. Those that don't care, or have bunkers themselves," the eldest maid concluded.

"What are you doing?" V asked them.

"We're going home."

Sal nodded in acceptance. "Hey!" he yelled to Nathan and Toemat who looked over to the group. "The fuck are you two doing?"

\*

Graced with another night in the woods, the gang decided to get a few tasks done. They were in Woodstock, making their way across Ontario. They planned to ride lakeshore to Toronto. Tomorrow they would arrive in *Hammer Town*. Hamilton was a big, fun, dangerous city to tramps, even if you were also in a bike gang. The Bacchus MC, formally the Red Devils, ran most of the streets. After holding Hamilton for sixty-five years, the Red Devils patched over to the second largest MC, only behind the Hells Angels, late in twenty-fourteen.

Toemat, Nathan, and V had the group's dirty clothes in a small laundry mat off of Dundas Street. Nathan and V were leaning on one of the washers, both exhausted from a day of riding. Adjacent to them was a small boy, looking up at them. They looked larger than life. V smiled at him, then gave Nathan a kiss on the cheek and walked over to Toemat, who was at the other end of the laundry mat.

"Hey," Nathan said to the boy.

"Hey," he said.

Nathan looked past the kid at his mom. She was on the phone yelling at someone, paying no attention to her son. "I don't care if the world is fucking ending! You still have to do your job-"

Nate squatted down and pulled a quarter out of his pocket. "Wanna see a magic trick?" he asked.

"Yeah," said the kid in a humble yet excited tone.

Nathan looked behind him to make sure V and Toemat couldn't see him, then held his hand out with the quarter on his palm. He began to levitate the quarter slowly, and watched the boy's eyes widen in disbelief. He took his hand away, leaving the quarter floating in place.

"Take it."

The kid slowly reached out, and plucked it out of the air.

"You can have it. It's a magic quarter, so don't lose it."

"I won't!" he said in a determined voice. He ran over to his mom's purse and pulled out a little plastic frog, then walked back to Nathan and gave it to him. "Here."

Nathan didn't expect that. It made him grin. "Thank you."

\*

# PART III
## Revelance
## (Anagnorisis)

# Chapter Ten:
## ~Hotel Lakeshore~

Thames River glistened to the rising sun. The deciduous trees had their buds, and grass had their dew. The morning light poked a hole in the shade and struck Nathan in the face. He awoke with crusty eyes, and to his disappointment, a terrible feeling of dread. The back of his eyes were stinging. What day was it? It was still June, but little else held to his memory. Why was he feeling this way? It seemed as though the trees and the water and the sky were all screaming at him to get up. To do something. Time was running out... How could he know that though? And why? Why was time running out? What was happening? He walked over to his bike and pulled the tarp off. He followed routine and folded it up, then put it in his soft top case on the back of the bike.

The gang woke up one by one. Toemat took a pee in the river. Sal took a swig of water from his canteen. V stretched and cracked every bone in her body. Sal looked over at Nathan's Ninja and frowned. He walked over to it and inspected the frog that was super glued to the Ninja's front fairing.

"Is this a plastic frog on your hood?" he asked.

Nathan huffed a laugh. "Yeah."

"A kid gave it to him at the laundromat," said V with a smirk.

"C'mon Greg," Toemat interrupted as he nudged Greg awake.

"Mmm. I'm up."

They hit the road, taking Dundas to highway fifty-three, and fifty-three to four-oh-three. There was next to no more traffic anymore. It meant to the group that Hamilton was only an hour away. The last time Nathan was in the Hammer was the day of his graduation, four years ago. The first time he talked to V. He told her about the dream he had...

'The dream that's now come true.'

After passing Ancaster, the gang took Lincoln M. Alexander Parkway to Upper James Street. After so long now, Nathan recalled that he still had his old iPod. It was in the inside pocket of his jacket. Could it still be alive? He pulled it out, switched off the lock, and it lit up. With next to no battery power in it, it could be the time he listened to his music. He popped the earbuds in while keeping his steering, and gave the iPod a shake. It was one of the ways to activate shuffle, and the song: *How*, by The Neighbourhood came on. It couldn't have picked a better song. He let it play, soaking in his surroundings, and watched Hamilton's downtown roll into view.

The cityscape was beautiful. The buildings and bridges and factories all meshed together and moulded into a concrete jungle; for humans, by humans. The gang parked at their usual spot, a bar off of Main Street East, and Nathan n' V decided to grab some packs. They walked into the close by convenience store, and V checked out the magazines.

Nathan walked up to the cashier. "Hey there."

"Hey, how are you doing?"

"Good, good... How are you? Not scared about the end of the world?" Nathan asked.

"End of the world? No. I've lived through many of those," the old black man said surprised. "I'm just a little tired."

"You doing okay?"

"Yeah yeah, I'm fine," he said with a chuckle. "Nothing to worry about. What can I do for you?"

"May I please get a carton offff... Next, blue, regular; please?"

The old man turned around and pulled out a carton, and exchanged with Nathan. Nathan was turning away, and the man interrupted.

"What's your name son?"

"Nathan."

"Nathan, has anyone ever told you that you have an old soul?"

"Not the people I hang out with."

"Most people don't realize what they're actually saying when they say it, but it's true. There are young souls and old. It's important to understand the influence past lives have on us. I can tell, you have been around for a long time," he said with a look of utter assertion.

"How do you know?" Nathan asked.

The man just smiled, and said, "You two have a good day."

"You too," said V, oblivious to their conversation. She grabbed the carton from Nathan. He didn't want to leave, but she put his arm over her and led them out.

They met up with Sal, Toemat and Greg at the bar, just as Sal had a few questions...

"Hey," he said with an up-nod.

"Hey," answered the bartender.

"This may be a stupid question but, what's the latest on the news? Is everybody really heading to the states?"

"Ain't that stupid of a question. You know how N.A.S.A. thought they had years to worry about it, then it just sped up like crazy? Well they're 'posed to hit any day now."

"Where is everybody running to then? Sounds kinda

unavoidable," said Toemat.

"South. The meteors are hittin' all around the top o' the Earth. I ain't leavin' though. I'm just gonna listen to the radio and bunker down when they come. Like the Hammer'll ever get hit anyway. Everyone's blown' this thing waaayyy out of proportion! It's just gonna be a few rocks. The size uh baseballs I bet."

"Eh. We'll see," said Sal.

Time passed. Toemat and V went out to do some shopping or something while the gang made the bar their home for the day. The bartender didn't mind, he actually preferred it. Nathan and Greg played pool, then Sal and Greg played pool, and Nathan lost again against Sal. Small groups of people came and went as the afternoon turned into night. Sal socialized to see what they had to say about the meteorites, and Greg and Nathan took another hand at the pool table. They teamed up against two young frat brothers from McMaster, and lost.

More time passed and Nathan found himself scrolling through his notebook, reliving some of the things he wrote in the past... Something, he had never done. He started at the very beginning.

-13/09/07-

'Dear Journal,
My name is Nathan, and I just created you. You're welcome. Today is going to be my first day in high school and I'm terrified. Zach and I are going to meet up at lunch and talk about our classes. Okay that's it, bye.

I'm back! The first day of high school has got to be the longest day I've ever had in my life. Zach and I had math together, and the rest of my classes had Vivian in them. I've had a crush on her since grade five. She has a button nose and wavy dark hair. She's the most beautiful girl I've ever seen. Sometimes it's too much to bare. Fuck. Why can't I talk to her?'

"Hmph," huffed Nathan, relapsing into nostalgia.

-13/10/24-

'Dear Journal,
Tomorrow is the Halloween dance and Vivian is going. She got popular now in high school. I really want to ask her to dance, but she probably doesn't like me. Zach isn't going and said it'd be stupid, but I want to go anyway.

-13/10/31-

Dear Journal,
So I don't know why I'm telling you this, but tonight I'm going to be alone. Zach doesn't want to hang out and watch scary movies like he said we would. I think he's hanging out with some other people. He didn't answer when I texted him, which makes me think he might be. He's been acting weird lately. Like distant.

-13/12/31-

The New Year approaches. Yay. So I've been trying to distract myself, but. Well Zach is no longer my friend. He hasn't been for a while. I don't know what to do. I've become so lonely. My brother and I have never gotten along, so I have absolutely no one.'

He scrolled the pages to a later date, and continued.

-15/08/24-

'Hey Journal long time no talk, and I guess for a good reason… Anyway I just got my G1. It took me six tries, but I finally got it. On the school front I have taken interests in art, gym and english. Grade eleven is fast approaching. It's strange that I'm already half-done high school. I didn't expect it would be like this. Anyway that is all for now.

-15/09/07-

Dear Journal,
Grade eleven here I come. No friends so far but who knows. There's still some hope for bullshit.

-15/11/21-

Dear Journal,
I can't sleep! In my mind I have no distractions, and I feel everything. Since I was born I could feel everything. The whole world opened up to me and it was too much to bear. Growing up I imagined myself fearless, but I'm grown now, and I know so much more.
How can any of us go on like everything is fine? We have no idea what we're doing half of the time, and then we die. Everything all at once is too much for anyone to bear. It scares me, but at the same time it makes me cry because of how beautiful it all is. My ego takes a beating, but I'll be fine. I'm fine.'

"Fuuuuck," Nathan mumbled to himself. His eyes were watering so he stopped. He was nothing like this person formally known as Nathan that he was reading. He couldn't believe it was his own writing. He was thinking about jumping back in, but Toemat and V entered the bar.

"Hayyee!" yelled Greg as he rushed in to bear hug Toemat. "What's it been, like six hours? What the fuck have you guys been up to?"

"Just sight-seeing," said V, before Toemat could say anything.

Sal left his new group to collect with everyone else. He and Toemat took the pool table. Greg talked to Toemat while he played, and V walked over to Nathan. She walked over with her hands together and a smile on her face that she was trying to suppress.

"Hey," said Nathan, finding her *very* attractive. She leaned in and gave him a kiss. "What's goin' on?"

"Mmm nothing, just missed you," she said, planting another kiss on his lips. She walked over to the bar to order a gin and tonic, and as she leaned over, her shirt lifted up a little… revealing bandages on the left side of her abdomen. Nathan pretended to watch the game of pool as V walked back over.

"Hey V, what do you got there?" Nathan asked as she took a seat. He lightly poked her side and she squirmed.

"Whaaaat? What do you got?"

She wriggled around before giving up and telling him. "I got it today with Toemat."

Nathan was grinning like a boy guessing what his Christmas presents were. "What is it?"

V lifted up her shirt, showing how big the actual bandage was. Nathan peeled it back slowly, to reveal a tattoo of the diamond pattern in his eyes.

"Whua-hahah-aaat?! Oh my God it looks just like it!" burst Nathan.

V was gleaming. "I made sure. I drew it the exact same."

He pressed the bandage down, and the two made out vigorously.

"See? I told yah," Toemat said to Greg, both of them grinning. The pool game was stopped to watch the show.

"Diamond eyes," said Sal with a grin and a shake of the head.

"Mm," said Nathan, interrupting their make out session, "I'll be right back."

"Kay."

He got up and rushed to the bathroom. V swivelled to face the group with the glass of gin in hand. "What?" she asked innocently, taking a sip.

Nathan was feeling strange again. He didn't feel feverish, but something was definitely going on. He felt a sting in the back of his eyes like from the morning, and it was getting stronger. He walked into the bathroom and took a piss at one of the urinals. He looked on at the wall in front of him, and his vision began to blur significantly. He blinked hard to try and fix his focus. It eventually faded back to normal on its own, leaving Nathan deeply concerned.

'What the fuck is happening to me.'

He washed his hands and returned to the group.

"Hey Nate!" bellowed Greg.

"Hey."

"So Nathan," said Sal as Nathan took his seat, "you know how we're taking Lakeshore to Toronto? Well everyone here is under the impression that most people are headed for the hills along with everyone else,"

"Yeah."

"And that got me thinking. A bunch of years ago the old gang and I did a little something we called: Hotel Lakeshore. It was stupid risky, but the payoff was beautiful. Now, with everything going on, I'm thinking we spend tonight as rich men!- And woman."

V raised her glass.

"..Yeah. Yeah; fuck yeah, I'm in! Hotel Lakeshore, that sounds awesome," Nathan answered with joy to the gang. V kissed him on the cheek. He held her close, and kissed her on the lips.

"I'll be right back," she said, reiterating Nathan. She

walked off to the bathroom, and Sal n' Toemat continued with their game. And at this time, wouldn't you know it, the feeling came back. Fuzzing consumed Nathan's skull. His vision blurred, then began to bubble outwards, like a picture painted on spandex. The centre of his vision stretched out, while the sides closed in. His surroundings wobbled, and everybody's energy sources began to glow from their chests. He couldn't control what was happening to him. He became a helpless victim to his own body. All sound became muffled as his surroundings morphed.

Toemat yelled out, "I, am, Spartacus!"

And Nathan's body slung forward at a tremendous rate, through the pool table to the other side of the bar. It ripped him violently from his trance and collided him into a large bearded man near the exit. His stomach was burning in the spot where he passed the table.

"What the fuck!?" the man yelled. He grabbed Nathan and hauled him outside, and his posse followed.

"Oh shit!" Sal yelled quick.

"How'd he get over there?!" asked Greg with no reply. Toemat had no idea but he at least knew that *something* was going.

His gang rushed out to meet him. V following quickly after.

"Look man I don't want any trouble. I don't even know what just happened," Nathan said in an attempt to reason.

The man pointed at Nathan and looked to his friends. "This fuckin' guy," he said as he turned around quickly and punched Nathan in the face, really hard. It whacked the lights out of him for a split second.

"DAWN REDWOOD!" Nate spat, with his head still hanging.

"What?" the combatant asked.

"Kick his ASS!" screamed Greg.

The man grabbed Nathan by his father's jacket and swung another punch. Nate dodged it this time. Everything was slowed now. He looked at the man, with his energy source showing. He retraced his failed swing... and Nathan punched him hard, straight into his nose. The man dropped, and his friends lunged in. One attempted a grab, but Nate side-stepped him and let the assailant hit the ground. Sal and Greg jumped in, eager to fight, and the six had themselves a brawl.

"Why aren't you jumping in?!" V asked Toemat.

"I'm not getting punched."

Nathan rapid-punched his combatant to the ground, unconscious, and jumped to help Greg who was on all fours. He tackled the man off of Greg and Greg got up to help Sal. Nathan stood as the man he tackled caught his stagger and stood his ground in a fighting pose, waiting for resistance. But Nate relaxed, and his pupils contracted. The man's heart was thumping out of his chest. He didn't know why the fight was halting.

"Whu-what the fuck?" he stuttered to Nate.

Sal and Greg walked up from behind Nathan and looked at the last opposing man standing in a state of opposition.

"C'mon," said Nate, "he's, uh, not a threat."

They were both confused, but took his advice in respect. They all walked past him. V ran up to Nathan and held his arm. Toemat ran over to the fallen men and looted their pockets for money.

"You still got it," V said to Nathan with an excited grin.

The last man standing watched as Toemat performed his malicious act, and was speechless. Toemat ran passed him to meet up with the others, leaving the man in shock, and the gang jumped on their bikes.

"Everyone watch for cops tonight," Sal said in a cautious but excited tone.

"We still doing Hotel Lakeshore?" asked Greg.

"We're still here! Might as well!" answered Sal.

Their engines roared to life. The feeling was to Nathan cathartic. He couldn't wait for what came next.

The gang hit the road with a mission. They took the Skyway to Brant Street, and carried on to Lakeshore. The streets were empty. It felt weird. Sal led the pack, with Nathan and V at the tail. They were riding at forty kilometres per hour, watching left and right for houses that looked accessible. Nathan peered right at one of the houses, and swerved into the driveway.

"Hey!" V shouted. She followed him up and the two got off their bikes. "What are we doing?" she asked.

Nathan walked up to the front door and peeled a sticky note off it. The gang rode up as he turned around. He had a big smirk on his face.

"Dude, what the fuck?" said Greg.

"It says: 'John we left the door unlocked. Your father and I have gone to California and as soon as you read this take a flight!'"

"OHHH!" screamed Greg. The gang collectively roared in delight.

"Okay, come on, come on," said Sal. They all walked their bikes around the gate to the backyard and peered through the windows to make sure someone wasn't already there.

The next moments were filled with merriment. They filed into the mansion and began raiding the fridge and jumping on the couches. Toemat ran downstairs to see if they had a wine cellar, and Nate n' V went upstairs to take a gander at the bedrooms. V led the way, giving Nathan a nice view of her strut. He patted her butt cheeks to hurry her up and they ran the rest of the way to the top. V took a room to the left. Nathan waited until she couldn't see him, then he opened a door on the right with his mind. He made the gesture of turning the knob and it did. Then he flicked a finger up, and the lights came on. He jumped on the bed in front of him, and lay for a moment. After so long, to lay in a bed was majestic. It was so God damned comfortable. He raised his head, and noticed a music player sitting on the cabinet in front of him. He got up and walked over to it.

"Hey," he called over to V.

He detached the iPad mini that was clicked in to it and brought the screen to life. The screen lock was titled: Lolita. He swiped it, hoping there was no password, and to his luck there was not.

"Oh my God, music!" said V as she entered the room.

"Yeah and look, you can choose like any song you want on here."

"Oh really…"

She took the iPad mini from his hands and casually pushed him back on the bed. Nathan leaned back and shrugged his jacket off while V scrolled through the songs, until she found the one. THE one. The song: *Fall In Love,* by Paradigm. It began to play through speakers in the walls. V lay the iPad down, and turned around with tiger eyes on Nathan…

She walked over to him with the beat, and swayed her hips from side to side. Another first for Nathan: getting a lap dance. Her body rocked to the music. She sat on his lap and grinded on him. He was getting hot, quick. She slipped off him as the song slowed, and began unbuckling his belt. Then Greg burst in.

"Hey you guys- Oh shit!" he slammed the door closed, "Sorry!" and rushed back downstairs.

Nate n' V's shock lulled and they both laughed.

"It's a strange love," said V as she got off her knees. She planted a kiss on his lips and rushed out of the room.

"Whoooe..." Nathan released. He latched his belt together, and covered his bruised torso again by his shirt.

Everyone sat around the dining table in their underwear waiting for Toemat to come in with the meal he made.

"While we all wait for our laundry," Toemat began as he entered the room, holding a silver tray, "may we all dine with some smoked trout, fava beans, garlic, lemon rind and pine nuts, dressed with extra virgin olive oil."

Everyone cheered him as he finished the meal's introduction.

"Wow!" said Greg. Toemat handed the meals out and everyone dug in.

"As always I am impressed," said Sal with his mouth full.

Nathan had a bite and was taken back. "This is delicious- Toemat I had no idea you were a cook."

He smirked and nodded his head, showing only to Nathan that he was being cautious with him. "Haven't been for a while..." He was proud of his dish, and watched on as the gang devoured it.

"So, none of us want to talk about it," Sal began to the group, "I get that, but there's a strong likely hood of us running into some shit in Toronto. There's no way we won't. People think the world is coming to an end; I haven't seen a single police cruiser in the last two days and I don't think that's a coincidence. Either we hit Toronto and the place is under government lockdown, or the city will be abandoned to the crazies. If the latter's the case, Skull will be right at home."

"Let's assume the former, we'll want to stay clear, right?" Toemat asked the table.

"Hell yeah," said Greg.

"We'll take our time getting there," Sal said as an answer. "We'll see."

The sky was still dark, but morning was coming. Nathan and V lay in bed together. They just performed the beast with two backs and were on their way to sleep.

"Hey Nathan," V said softly. He quietly grumbled to let her know he was listening. "I love you… so, much."

He opened his eyes and they stared at each other. "I've been in love with you since the moment I saw you, twelve years ago. It's the most obvious thing I've ever known."

She wiggled as close as she could to him, and slipped her legs in between his. They kissed each other long and soft.

"You're the love of my life," said V. She stroked his cheek, and a tear rolled down her face. Nathan wiped it away and kissed her again.

"You're the love of mine… You're the only one, forever."

\*

# Chapter Eleven:
## ~The Big City~

Feelings, were feeling fleeting. New nuances nestled neatly near frank, fussed frickle-fracks. Nonsense in the nothing began to slip and slide into sense and something… A sound could be heard. It was faint, but getting clearer. Wind. Winds were blowing. Sight came into view. There were rolling hills of green, blown grass. In the distance a metallic object slid across the sky like a figure skater. The view had a slow rolling tracking shot. It faded to concrete hills. The day turned to night, and Nathan was heading down a street. His eyes took a tight right turn that led him into a tunnel. In he went, and all went black. The set inside the tunnel illuminated. It was his old high school cafeteria. There were students everywhere. Nathan retracted from the back of his head and watched on as the hustle and bustle of lunch time commenced. He could feel the sorrowful plunge of nostalgia mix into the chemical cocktail of his mind.

At the end of the room a group of girls sat at a round table, talking and laughing with each other. One of them was Vivian. Nathan tried to call out to her but he had no voice. His body stood at the doors looking onward, and people began to disappear one by one. V looked over at him and their eyes locked. Then it changed. All the remaining students, the tables and chairs, all disappeared. The daytime light dimmed, and to Nathan's horror… a skeletal man on horseback appeared behind V. He was armour-clad except for the skull. Lava spit out of the openings of the amour and spilled onto the floor. He held a mace, and with one swift spin, flung the spiked ball at V. She didn't turn around, didn't see him. The mace struck her and she let out a scream, at the same time, puffing into ash.

A horrific chorus of fallen angels erupted, and the man he-ahed his horse into a charge at Nathan. He was still frozen like a corpse in rigamortis. The inside of his head was on fire with emotions. Shock, fear, desperation, anger, depression and anxiety all boiled together as the mace swung and the horse galloped. The horseman passed him and circled back around.

'Did anything happen?!'

He looked down, and the left side of his abdomen was gashed open and bleeding out. He didn't feel any pain, but the sight was mortifying. The horseman charged again. Flames licked the lava as it spurt out of him and his horse. He swung his mace up and knocked Nathan off of his feet. Nathan collapsed into water, and looked up. He could see the nighttime sky. He could see the full moon. The moon seized him and suspended him out of the water and into space. In seconds Nathan was slung at the moon until he was above the surface. On the surface, directly at the centre of his vision, was a vantablack rectangular prism. The possible culprit?

"NATHAN!"

His eyes burst open, and he dropped onto the bed. V was clenching the blanket in horror. Nathan looked at her, and was speechless. She just witnessed him levitating, what could he say? He got up and began pacing the end of the bed.

"What… what."

"I… th-that's, never happened before… not that I know of," Nathan responded in lame.

"Then why are you not as shocked as I am?"

Nathan hesitated before saying, "I've been… I've been starting to," he whispered, "move, things, with my mind."

"You're fucking with me. Why are you fucking with me? I just saw you floating in the fucking air!"

"Shhh!"

"Are you, like, possessed, or something?"

"No I'm not possessed V, come on," he said with a frown. They both let their racing hearts slow down, and Nate took a seat on the bed. That was when footsteps marched from outside to their door where Toemat swung it open to confront whatever situation was going on inside.

"Jesus Toemat, you don't have to stick your nose in this."

The response Nathan gave lit a flame in Toemat. "You're damn right I don't, but that's exactly what I'm going to do!"

Greg was in the main floor bedroom but the ruckus upstairs was enough to wake him up and send him to investigate. Sal was in the basement bedroom, blissfully unaware of the noise allowing him to sleep contently. Greg marched into Nathan and V's room to find Toemat, flustered, standing at the door opposite to the two on the bed.

"Toemat seriously what the fuck are you doing?"

"This whole scene is getting out of hand," said Nathan.

"Tell me why it shouldn't!" Toemat yelled.

"Toemat!" Nathan barked in a whisper, "You want everyone in this room? At least give Sal the peace of ignorance."

"Is that you confessing?" he asked.

Greg still stood completely confused as to what the situation was at all.

"That me confessing?" Nathan said with a short fuse due to embarrassment. He grabbed his notebook that he had on the nightstand and threw it at Toemat. "Here. Here's me fucking confessing."

Both Toemat and Greg scrutinized the notebook as Toemat flipped to the most recent pages with the latest entries. "T.V.M.?" he questioned out loud.

"Bullshit," Greg said as his conclusion.

"I wouldn't believe me either."

Nathan paused for a moment, then raised his hand to the nightstand beside V. The lamp on it began to gently wobble before levitating an inch into the air. V let out a gasp. He lowered it back down and looked at the ground. The group was speechless. "I need you guys to get out of here. I need to talk to V alone, if that's okay," Nathan said rather bluntly but with the slightest courtesy. Toemat and Greg remained standing on the spot, still in shock. Greg made the first move by turning around and walking like a zombie out of the room. Toemat followed behind him and closed the door on his way out. Nathan then look to V.

"You remember that dream I had? First time we talked?"

"Of us riding motorcycles together down the highway," she answered. "You didn't remember how it ended."

"I think I do now. We ride east. Spend the summer as the People's Deviants then leave. Sal would understand. We can sell our bikes and settle down somewhere. We've walked farther. Got to know more, and grow more. We've felt less, but now it's time to further our walk. We have each other now."

V looked into his eyes and saw the shimmer. How could she say no?

*

The team prepared themselves with the rising sun by

packaging all the food they could in their bags, sacs and pockets. The home owners' son never arrived in their stay. The front door opened with everyone casually talking to each other as they exited, and in Nathan's troubled mind the song: *What a Difference a Day Makes*, by Dinah Washington played. Previously he wrote one last passage in his journal. The passage read as such:

-//-

'The synapses in my mind have just now finally given me a memory of my childhood of bliss. I remember poking my head out of a pile of leaves to surprise my parents in our front lawn. I must have been four. The sun has a strange way of poking itself out from the horizon to surprise us all every morning. It always seems to go slow when you focus on it but look away and in the blink of an eye everything around you is as bright as its maker. The planet slings around the star with a dizzying spin and we all go in and out of focus. What really matters in the end? My attention is with V but it keeps being pulled at to look towards the future. This gang of brothers will fall apart, the stars will rain fire, and I will hold V's hand. How selfish of me. I wish I could just go back, knowing everything I know now and take my time; but this is life, and you can never go back.'

The sun made its way down the vacant mansions' walls as the morning worked its way into the day. Street signs flew by as the gang rode through the ghost town of what was once Burlington. It was always bustling in the morning. The dramatic change left an unsettling pit in Nathan's gut. He was born in this city, and now it was a stranger to him. They rolled into a gas station at the edge of town to fill up before Toronto. Sal got off his twenty-twelve Harley and jogged over to the station, but the doors were locked.

"What?" Toemat asked after Sal shook the handles.

"It's locked."

"What time is it?" Greg asked.

"We left at like ten, there's no way it's actually closed," said V.

"Well what are we supposed to do now?" Sal asked as he walked back over to the group.

Nathan furrowed his brow in concern as he began to remember something.

"What?" Vivian asked him.

"What's the date today?"

"The twenty fourth?" said Sal, posing it as a question though he knew.

"Why?" asked Greg while Toemat walked over to the doors.

"V, we graduated on the twenty fifth, right?"

"Yeah…"

"Beware the quartern of year…" Nathan mumbled to himself.

"What's going on?" V asked. She looked very concerned. Then Toemat shattered a window and opened the station, breaking the tension in the air.

"C'mon!" he yelled in excitement.

Nathan put his hand on V's shoulder. "We're fine, we'll just get to Toronto."

The gang spent the better part of the morning and afternoon gallivanting the abandoned malls and plazas. Street racing into parks and spinning donuts were just some of the activities. There were others they ran into on the streets but not many. The people had the same level of enthusiasm as the gang, treating the town like it were their own. When passing residential neighbourhoods on the way to the big city Nathan noticed draped in windows shutting quickly. The faces were mostly older people. As the sun continued it journey down the west side of the sky dome the fun subsided. It was the dream of any nihilistic deviant to society but the group were not full of children, and they had places to be. Sal led everyone up Trafalgar road from Cornwall to the on ramp for the four-oh-three highway. The gang hit the highway on bound to Toronto and met absolutely no traffic, in either direction.

"Keep an eye out for cops or military," Sal mentioned as Greg played with the lanes, zigzagging and popping wheelies. Nathan looked over at V. She was happy and so was he, but she looked worried. He knew all that fun couldn't make her forget about what she saw. Toemat and Greg were taking it fine but he could tell it was hard for them to not say anything in the presence of Sal.

"There it is!" Toemat shouted.

Nathan looked onward. The Mississauga buildings were gone now, and Toronto's were rising. The Canadian National tower was visible from Burlington but with it so close it seemed to pierce the heavens.

"Hope it doesn't rain," Sal called out.

Nathan looked in his side mirrors then twisted his head behind him. A thick sheet of large storm clouds had been sneaking up behind them the whole time, rolling in as a tag-along. They all sped on, into the big city. High-rise buildings engulfed them, and they took an off ramp which finally put them into Toronto, in all its glory. Skyscrapers scraped the sky in every direction. It was like nothing Nathan had ever seen before. His breath was taken away looking up at all the buildings.

"This is so incredible," he exhaled.

V looked over at him and smiled.

The gang hit a red light and everyone looked around. "The latter then," said Toemat.

Their intersection was deserted but in the distance, they could hear screaming and cheering, undoubtedly people doing the same thing they were doing earlier. To Nathan's right was an electronic store, showcasing televisions. On every T.V. was the same broadcast: a news report about the current event: the meteors.

"The object," the news lady began, "that was found orbiting close to the sun," an image popped up showing a gif of a circular object with a semi-circle gap at the bottom, right next to the sun, being hit with solar flares, "has now locked orbit with the Earth's rotation. It leads many astronomers to believe the object in question may have something to do with the current trajectory and velocity of the incoming meteorites. What they mean by that is unclear at this time."

Nathan was watching intently as everyone else saw the light turn green and accelerated.

"Nathan it's green!" V called out. He didn't look away, just moved his bike to the curb.

"We'll meet you at Caz and boys; at two-thousand and one," said Sal to V, understanding that Nathan was fixated.

"The meteorite warning is in affect tonight. Minimal damage is expected, but you are required to stay indoors or underground if you can, until it subsides. This is Meredith Farcz, for News Six."

"Come on Nathan," said V.

He turned away from the broadcast slowly, and looked at V, with a dreaded face.

'What the fuck am I supposed to do?'

\*

V and Nathan arrived at two-thousand and one, the address of what appeared to be an abandoned building in a run-down part of the city. Street lights came on, letting them know that it was nighttime now. On the brick wall opposite to them was a spray paint piece of art that said: DON'T BE FOOLED with an eye looking up and meteorites falling past the pupil.

There appeared to be just a garage door. V knocked on it.

"Whatchu doin'?" asked Toemat on the other side.

"Chillin' with the crickets," said V, reciting the code phrase, and he opened up. The whole ground floor was a parking garage. The only other people there were Sal and Greg.

"Isn't this someone else's hangout?" Nathan asked Toemat as he and V rolled in.

"Yeah," said Sal as he scratched the back of his head.

"You don't think they left?" V asked.

Nate took his helmet off. "The news is being quaint. This thing is bigger than a few rocks hitting down. It's serious."

"Mhn, you got a point diamond eyes. I mean, Caz and his gang move like clockwork. They're always here right when the street lights come on," Sal continued.

"Where do you think they'd be otherwise?" asked Nathan.

Sal gave a face that said, 'I don't know,' then Toemat piped in.

"That one bar in Newmarket?"

"It's worth checking out. You guys stay here, I'll head out with Nate," said Sal. He pointed to the garage door, "Keep that door locked tight while we're gone. If shit's as crazy as it seems then people might try and break in looking for shelter or cars or something."

V held Nathan's arm tightly.

"We'll be back before you know it. It'll be fine," he said.

"That's not what I'm worried about," said V without an explanation. She kissed him and they hugged, then he slid his helmet on and followed Sal out the garage door.

"If we're not back in two hours then come to us," said Sal. He started up his Harley and Nathan his Ninja. But before Nate could take off with Sal Greg grabbed his sleeve. Nathan looked at him.

"Just, show me one more time," he whispered. Nate looked at Sal who revved his engine while scooting forward to say 'let's go', so he quickly aimed his powers down at Greg's left pant leg and pulled it up with force. In the following second his ninja rode away and Sal went up to take the lead, and the two were off.

\*

The skies were dense with clouds, blocking any moonlight from getting through. The city lights reflected off the clouds, giving them a menacingly dim orange. The plastic frog came in and out of illumination from the street lights as Nathan and Sal rode. The met their destination and rolled up to the bar. Three motorcycles were parked at the entrance.

"Huh," said Sal.

"What?" asked Nathan.

"Those aren't their bikes."

\*

# Chapter Twelve:
## ~Genesis~

Toemat rolled onto his belly, and got up off the floor. "Has it been two hours yet?"

"Hasn't even been one," said Greg with his eyes closed.

-BAM BAM BAM-

Greg, V, and Toemat all flinched.

"Jesus!" said V.

"Whatchu doin'?" shouted Toemat. A flashlight shone through the underbelly of the garage door. "Who's shining?"

"Toemat?! It's Lyndon man, let me in!"

Toemat hoisted up the garage door, and Lyndon stumbled in.

"Close it!" he hissed. Lyndon looked beaten to a pulp. His face was all bruised and bloodied up.

Greg was mortified. "Holy shit."

Toemat slammed the door down and Greg blurted out, "Lyndon what the fuck happened to you?"

"It's Skull man! He's got a new gang now and they're wiping us all out! He shot Caz right in front of me man." Lyndon's lips were quivering as he continued. "I ran off and hid till I couldn't hear them anymore... then came here, hoping others made it... but I think I'm the only one." He collapsed to his knees and sobbed into his hands.

"Jesus, Lyndon..." V walked over and put a hand on his shoulder. Everyone else was speechless.

Lyndon wiped the tears and snot from his face, then continued. "There aren't any cops out or anything. The streets have gone to the dogs."

The group sat in silence. What were they to make of

this?

-TSH!-

The garage door whipped up. Bright biker lights stunned the gang. Three silhouettes could be seen in front of the lights. They pulled out guns. Toemat pulled out his, but before he could fire, he was shot… twice in the chest. Greg was shot in the leg and dropped. V screamed and dropped into the fetal position. Toemat collapsed on the ground, dead. Greg dragged himself to Toemat's body in a desperate attempt to grab his gun. A man walked up to him on the ground, and pointed a gun at his head.

-BANG-

Smoke slid out the barrel of the gun. The man holding the gun, was non-other, than Skull. He walked over to Lyndon, who was a shaking petrified mess on the ground.

"Thanks for bringing us to your new den," he said, then pointed his gun at Lyndon and pulled the trigger.

The gunshot made V flinch through her shaking. She lowered her hands down, and Skull walked up to her. He squatted down and stared at her. He didn't say anything, but a big wide grin was on his face. V already knew what he was thinking. He gently slid his hands into her armpits and lifted her up. They stood facing each other, while the other two bikers with Skull stood back and watched. V made a quick reach for her Jungle King hunting knife, and swung it hard at Skull's upper torso. Skull smacked the back of her wrist, releasing the knife, and he backhanded her. She spun in the air and hit the ground, landing on her face. She lay, defeated. Skull got on his knees and began unbuckling his belt…

\*

Sal and Nathan entered the bar. It was musty with smoke. People sat in pews, all looking burnt out. The bartender looked to the door in desperation as they entered, maybe hoping for the police, or anyone that could help.

"I don't like this," Nathan grumbled under his breath.

Sitting at the bar stools were three men drinking beer. Nate presumed they were the bikers. The men looked over at Sal and Nathan, and finished their drinks. The song: *The Man Comes Around,* by Johnny Cash was playing while they stood in deadlock at the entrance. They didn't know what to do. Nate was hoping Sal would say something, but he just stood there and waited.

The three men got off their stools, and drew guns. Sal's eyes widened. Nathan's pupils ballooned. In the second that transpired, the men shot at them… One bullet hit the door. One hit Sal in the chest, and one grazed Nathan's arm. The men shot again, hitting Sal in the shoulder. He whipped back and hit the ground. The other two bullets hit the door.

"What the fuck?" one of the men called out.

"Where did he go?"

"What the fuck was that?"

"Where did he just FUCKING go?!"

Nathan appeared again where he just was, but this time holding a double barrel shotgun. He emptied both barrels in an instant, with barely any recoil. The first shell hit the left biker's shooting arm, and the second blasted and tore a chuck out of another's leg. The last man standing unloaded his clip at Nathan in terror. Nate weaved and dodged the bullets while moving closer to the assailant, and knocked him unconscious by upper-cutting him with the shotgun. The other two men lay screaming in pain on the ground. The patrons of the bar were silent in fear for their lives. Nathan dropped the gun and ran to Sal.

"Jesus, Sal!" Nathan yelled franticly, but he was gone. "No, no no no no no. Oh fuck-" He gasped.

'V!'

He slung himself outside, whipped a leg over his Ninja, and then slung away with it.

\*

In Edmonton, in the office of Mark Hamilton, the district manager of an arborist company, the door remained locked like it always did in the evening. But somehow, his double barrel shotgun vanished, and his desk had a hole horribly warped in the middle.

\*

The streets of Toronto were loud now. There were people and fires on almost every street. Nathan reappeared at the gang base and jumped off his Ninja. Two thousand and one's garage door was open at the bottom. It wasn't a good sign. He slung the door away, and walked inside...

"No... Noo, nooo. Nooo! NOOO! NOOOOOO!!!"

The horrific, gruesome death scene was laid out in front of him more graphic than any police forensic photographs. V was at the back of the room, on the ground like everyone else. Nathan's vision went blurry. His eyes filled with tears. He stumbled over to her body and fell to his knees.

"V... Veeeeee," he grumbled through his crying.

Nathan hugged her and sobbed, rocking back and forth. Then something happened. Something he was not prepared for or wanted in any measure. The back of his head inflamed, and his vision was stolen. He began to see and hear blurred and muffled things. He saw V's hands covering his sight. They lowered and a man walked over to him, and squatted down in front of him. He had a big grin on his face, and Nathan knew who it was. It was Skull.

His senses came back to him. He could hear rain pouring outside. He rested V on the ground again, with shaking hands. His heart was beating a mile a minute, and his breathing deepened.

"Skull… did, this…"

Nathan's head was on the verge of exploding. His blood boiled, curdled, and solidified in his veins. His organs stopped, and that was it. Out went his humanity, his everything, his nothing. He was barely holding onto life as it was. V was his tether, and the tether was cut, releasing Nathan's soul into the void. Bleak, pale emptiness rushed into his heart and his tear-well dried up. He had no more for this world to take. Now it was his turn. With nothing to lose, and under his own volition, he would go out to the streets and find Skull. He would find him and he would kill him, slowly, painfully. Then he himself would lay down to die.

Nathan began to feel faint from the heavy breathing so he closed his eyes for a moment. As he opened them he spoke to his dead love.

"I had the strength to do anything when I was with you. If it's the last thing I do, I'll kill Skull for you." He stood up and walked out into the rain. He got on his Ninja, and rode off.

There were a lot more people out now. Fires were in trashcans. Every store window was shattered. People who weren't in the stores looting, were under canopies hiding from the rain. A group of guys were huddled near the corner of an intersection around a flaming trashcan, waiting for the rain to subside. They watched as Nathan rolled by. He turned right on the corner, and one of the guys ran into the store beside him. He came riding out on a motorcycle and rolled around the corner to chase down Nathan, but it was a trap. Nathan stood waiting on the sidewalk, and as soon as the man turned the corner, Nathan lifted his hand up. The guy's motorcycle was flung from under him and launched high into the air, landing him on his ass.

"Ahhh!" he screamed out in pain and disbelief.

Nathan walked up to him slowly, and stood over him. The man's motorcycle crashed down, making him flinch. Nathan stood unmoved.

"Go get Skull," he said.

The bruised biker stumbled backwards, terrified, and ran away.

The clouds still covered the night sky like a blanket, but the rain trickled, until it was no more. Nathan waited at the intersection, beside his bike. Crowds gathered but were afraid to do anything, so they stood on the sidewalks and talked to themselves as they waited too. The low hum of motorcycles began to fill the air. It got louder, and louder. The crowd was getting excited. They knew they were in for something big. The hum turned into a roar, and out of a side street, Skull's gang appeared. Bike after bike filed in, until the other side of the intersection was filled with gang members. They got off their bikes and walked up to the line. There must have been about fifty men. Nathan looked at them all, searching the faces for Skull. Then he appeared, rolling his Harley to the front. The two looked at each other in silence, for hours of seconds.

"So you're the guy fuckin' my men up!" Skull shouted out. Nathan said nothing. "They say you got superpowers! They say you're the devil! And you want me? I'm honoured!"

"...You killed V!!!"

"Not before I finally got mine!"

The gang behind him roared in hysterical, disgusting applause and Nathan raised his extended hand at Skull. He thought about blowing his head up, but he lowered his hand instead and closed his eyes.

'Dawn Redwood,' he whispered in his head.

His vision expanded, and everything became translucent. The people around him all had glowing lights in their chests, and the ground... The ground was on fire, like the Earth was screaming. A speaker system in one of the stores began blasting the song: *The Final Cut*, by 501. He opened his eyes as the vibrations washed over everyone, and the opposing men ran at Nathan. The fight began.

Without using manipulation, Nate took the men head on. He beat them down with extreme speed and force, one after the other. No one stood a chance against his heightened mindset. They came at him with knives and batons, and Nathan gave them a match like no one man had ever done... but it was not to no avail. As the number of fighters dropped Nathan speed began to slow. One man planted his knife in Nate's shoulder. He let out a yell of pain and the crowd began to question what they were watching. Nathan kicked the man in the chest and another man sliced him deep in the leg, dropping him onto his knee. At this point Nathan had enough and seized the remaining men where they stood. He dropped them hard into the ground and the onlookers erupted in panic. They all fled for their own protection out of fear.

Nathan's exhausted heartrate lulled, and his pupils contracted. Everyone was defeated; everyone, but Skull. He rode away while Nathan was fighting.

"That son of a bitch," he slurred to himself upon noticing.

He levitated himself up into the air until he could see all the streets without the buildings blocking him, and there he was. Skull and two others were riding away with haste maybe six blocks away. Nathan pointed his two front fingers at Skull and slung him back to the intersection, without his Harley. Then Nate slung himself back down.

"AHH! Ahhh, ahhhhh," Skull screamed as he looked all around him, baffled and bewildered. "You are the fuckin' devil," he said to his enemy as Nathan limped over and stood above him. "Fight me. Fight me or I'll kill you right now-"

With a quick lunge, Skull stabbed Nathan in the abdomen. His eyes bulged. He reached out to stop it, but wasn't prepared. He looked down, and saw the handle…

'V's Jungle King…'

"AUGHHH!!!" Nathan screamed as he threw Skull in the air. Skull landed down hard, breaking his right leg. He yelled in pain, then tried to get up and run. Nathan held him down on the ground and limped over to him, with his back curled over in pain. The other knife was still lodged in his back shoulder as he pulled the knife out slowly, spitting as he breathed, then sat on top of Skull.

'I'm going to kill him. I'm going to kill him.'

He placed his hand on Skulls face, and held the knife over him. Skull lay helpless and terrified, knowing his end was coming. But then, as Nathan held his hand on Skulls face, the back of his head inflamed again, and he lost sight.

"Nnnn! Nnnn!" Skull squealed through his teeth, wondering what was going on. Nathan froze on top of him. Then after a moment, he fell backwards.

Skull began to worm his way up and Nathan hovered the knife at Skulls face which made him stop.

"...WELL?!" Skull burst, making Nathan flinch. "Just fuckin' kill me."

Nathan shook his head aggressively as he was still in excruciating pain. "…No."

"What do you mean no?! Fucking kill me! You're gonna fucking kill someone, fucking do it!"

"Killing!," Nathan began, "is a symbolic solution… to a biological limitation."

The quote came from Ernest Becker's: The Denial of Death, one of the many books Nathan read in his time of solitude. He flung the Jungle King off down the street.

"What? What the fuck is that supposed to mean?"

"I'm not gonna fuckin' kill you. I'm not you." He got up, while holding his stab wound, and began to walk over to his Ninja.

"I know you're not me. I'm one of a fuckin' kind. I'm a full metal jacket wearing' mother fucker, you little SHIIIT!" Skull screamed out as Nate walked away.

"Nathan," whispered the woman in his head. It was her, the one from Europa: Synophy.

"Synophy! Oh no."

Loud sirens bellowed from the city streets. He looked up to the clouds, and to his horror a thing pushed the clouds down. A giant superstructure revealed itself from above. Kilometres across, a flat surface best described as a short, opened pincer with the texture of bone descended slowly and silently. Then a booming sound erupted from the floating structure, and a charging. The underbelly started to glow deep red, and the noise -YAHWEH- screeched the air! The sirens continued their panicked wail, and the red glow burst open. Light beamed straight down. In the utter instant impact, Nathan slung himself away.

Winds blew, and the sound of thousands screaming

could be heard in the distance. Nathan was free falling with the highway below him. His bike was in the air too. He slung himself to his bike, then slowed down their descent before touching ground. Where was he, Burlington? It was hard for him to focus on anything. He needed to inspect his flesh wounds. He unzipped his jacket and lifted his shirt. The abdomen wound was gushing blood. He put his shirt back down and began to sob. Everything was gone, and he could have stopped it. He could have stopped this if only he listened to Synophy…

His sobbing was interrupted as two jets flew over his head. They soared off eastbound, to Toronto. He could hear the delayed wind-rip as they went out of view… Then the sky lit up. It was a bomb. A big one. Nathan could see the mushroom cloud rise up in the parting clouds.

'Oh no!'

He had to get away, fast. He slung himself continuously. The surroundings stretched thinner and thinner the longer he slung. Then he broke out of it, and he was in free fall again. Where was he though? It was morning. Mountains were on his left and nothing but white was on his right. The ground was pitch-

-CSH-

He hit ice, really hard. He couldn't see how close the surface was because his eyes were still adjusting. Nathan and his Ninja plunged down into the ice-cold depth of some body of water. His bike sunk away, its headlight flickering as it died.

'Am I going to die?' Nathan thought to himself in panic. He didn't want to die, but he was so woozy. Sleep was taking him.

'No. No!'

He fell, deeper and deeper. His Ninja hit something

and made a -TNK- noise, like it hit against something else metal, and its lights went off. Everything was black.

'What did it hit?' Nathan thought to himself, drowsy and dizzy; and dying. Whatever it was, he was getting close. His foot scraped his bike, then kept going... or did it? It felt as if he didn't have a foot anymore. Was his bike above him now? Nathan directed his focus downward. It now seemed as if he wasn't underwater anymore.

Silence.

Silence.

Silence inside silence.

Silence without silence.

Utter, raw, nothing...

And then there was a change.

Noise. Wind. Winds. Loud winds! Blistering winds! Light! Bright light! Blinding light! It was everywhere! Not just forward, up, down, left and right, but everywhere! And everything! Everything was everywhere! Spilling and filling every crevice was light and dust and stars and galaxies. They were all as big and small as everything else. And everything was taking place at the same time! The big bang, chemicals, life, love. It was all happening at once and not at all. In the instant Nathan had it!... it was gone. Black. Then a sharp crack! And out Nathan flew.

He was floating outside his old house. Without direction, Nathan went through the walls, and there he was in bed, sleeping. Nathan went inside himself, and burst awake.

"Ah!" he screamed before silencing himself. He was huffing like he just ran the twelve-minute.

He looked down at his hands. They were skinny, and soft.

"Oh my God... Oh my God."

He looked at himself in his mirror, and it was his

eighteen-year-old self looking back at him.

"What the fuck…" he breathed to himself, wide-eyed and starry.

He couldn't move. He wouldn't move. He had to sit on his bed until any of this computed.

"Was it all a dream? No, it couldn't have been. It happened, I know it did… There was something… at the bottom of that lake… No it doesn't make sense. When I had that dream. When my eyes change."

And so, he sat. At six his alarm went off, and he slammed the snooze then took a deep breath.

"Okay Nathan what the fuck are you gonna do?"

He had to move. The plan was coming to him, he just had to move. He had to get up, and MOVE!

Nate pounced up, got dressed, and snuck into his parent's room. A little wooden box full of cash lay under his father's dresser. He slid it out, slowly and quietly, then hurried downstairs. With a pen and pad he wrote: 'If you ever want to see Nathan again, all three of you will get a room at the Quality Hotel and wait for further instructions.'

Then he took his parent's car keys and went out the door. The car rolled down the driveway and onto the street, silently, before Nathan turned the car on and drove away. He pulled into the Timmy's parking lot, and walked inside. V was standing at the counter with a smile on her face.

"No bike today?" she asked.

Nathan walked in behind the counter, shocking her and the other employees, and gave her a hug.

"Whu-" she was about to begin, then he kissed her on the lips.

"I love you, V."

She stood silent and still, completely bewildered.

"I won't be going to graduation because of something

very important I have to do, but I want you to meet me, whenever you can. I'll be in a little town I've been to before called Dymond. It's up Ontario. I know a guy there who can help me."

He looked at her shocked face and felt guilty. "I'm sorry it took me so long to tell you how I feel. Here, I wrote the name of the place down."

She took the sticky note from him. He kissed her one last time, and then left.

The sun was starting to rise. Nathan turned the radio up. The song: *Be Still,* by The Killers was playing. He looked on at the wide, long road ahead of him, and took a deep breath. He'd have to get rid of the car by seven.

'Is this supposed to be destiny or something? Or just coincidence?' he thought as he looked at himself in the mirror before grumbling to himself. "Destiny or coincidence; maybe it's both."

'Whatever it is I'm going in, eyes wide, though I don't know into what... But I intend to find out.' After a moment of silence, he sighed one last time. "At least I have time now. I just hope it's enough..."

**

# Songs of Deviance

Etude - - - - - - - - - - - - - - - - - - - - - - - Nero

What a Difference a Day Makes -  Dinah Washington

Between The Raindrops - - - - - - - Lifehouse

Back to The Shack - - - - - - - - - - - - - Weezer

My God Is the Sun - Queens Of The Stone Age

Seasons - - - - - - - - - - - - - - - - Future Island

Arabesque One Piano Solo - - - - - - Debussy

Ruby - - - - - - - - - - - - - - Twenty One Pilots

Beast Infection - - - - - - - - - - - - - - Grimes

Red Giant - - - - - - - - - - - - - - - - Stellardrone

Dreams - - - - - - - - - - - - - - - The Cranberries

Kangaroo Court - - - - - - - - - - - Capital Cities

How - - - - - - - - - - - - - - - - The Neighborhood

Fall in Love - - - - - - - - - - - - - - - -Phantogram

The Man Comes Around - - - - - Johnny Cash

The Final Cut - - - - - - - - - - - - - - - - - 501

Be Still - - - - - - - - - - - - - - - - - The Killers

# Nathan's Journal

*

Dear Journal,
My name is Nathan, and I just created you. You're welcome. Today is going to be my first day in high school and I'm terrified. Zach and I are going to meet up at lunch and talk about our classes. Okay that's it, bye.

I'm back! The first day of high school has got to be the longest day I've ever had in my life. Zach and I had math together, and the rest of my classes had Vivian in them. I've had a crush on her since grade five. She has a button nose and wavy dark hair. She's the most beautiful girl I've ever seen. Sometimes it's too much to bare. Fuck. Why can't I talk to her.

-13/10/24-

Dear Journal,

Tomorrow is the Halloween dance and Vivian is going. She got popular now in high school. I really want to ask her to dance, but she probably doesn't like me. Zach isn't going and said it'd be gay, but I want to go anyway.

-13/10/31-

Dear Journal,
So I don't know why I'm telling you this, but tonight I'm going to be alone. Zach doesn't want to hang out and watch scary movies like he said we would. I think he's hanging out with some other people. He didn't answer when I texted him, which makes me think he might be. He's been acting weird lately. Like distant.

-13/12/31-

The New Year approaches. Yay. So I've been trying to distract myself, but. Well Zach is no longer my friend. He hasn't been for a while. I don't know what to do. I've become so lonely. My brother and I have never gotten along, so I have absolutely no one.

-14/01/01-

Happy New Year, Journal.

I have never been kissed.

-15/08/24-

Hey Journal long time no talk, and I guess for a good reason... Anyway I just got my G1. It took me six tries, but I finally got it. On the school front I have taken interests in art, gym and English. Grade eleven is fast approaching. It's strange that I'm already half-done high school. I didn't expect it would be like this. Anyway that is all for now.

-15/09/07-

Dear Journal,
Grade eleven here I come. No friends so far but who knows. There's still some hope for bullshit.

-15/10/23-

Dear Journal,
My dad promised me that if I got a good grade on my accounting test that he would take time off work and the two of us would go to Fear Fest in Canada's Wonderland. AND WE'RE GOING! I can't wait. I don't know why but there's always been something about the autumn season that's made me feel warm with anticipation. And Halloween has always been my absolute favourite holiday, making today beyond exciting for me!

-15/11/13-

Some kid tried to start shit with me today at lunch for no reason. He followed me for a while. I tried to walk away from him. He kept calling me a loser and a fagot. I don't get it. That attack came out of nowhere. If it happens again I'm gunna punch him out.

-15/11/21-

Dear Journal,
I can't sleep! In my mind I have no distractions, and I feel everything. Since I was born I could feel everything. The whole world opened up to me and it was too much to bear. Growing up I imagined myself fearless, but I'm grown now, and I know so much more.
How can any of us go on like everything is fine? We have no idea what we're doing half of the time, and then we die.

Everything all at once is too much for anyone to bear. It scares me, but at the same time it makes me cry because of how beautiful it all is. My ego takes a beating, but I'll be fine. I'm fine.

-16/01/01-

Dear Journal,

Happy New Year! It's just my mom and I this time. My dad's overseas for business. My mom got Chinese food for the two of us and Alex, but he hasn't been home for two days. I've been noticing recently that my mom doesn't really have friends. Is that normal for adults? Anyway, there was more Chinese food for me so fuck yeah.

-16/02/14-

Dear Journal,

Like I'm in any position to talk to Vivian, let alone give her a Valentine's Day card. But I made one for her anyway. She has hundreds of friends and probably a jacked jock boyfriend, and I've got no one. I don't even think I know how to talk to people anymore. Well whatever. I don't even know what I'm writing anymore.

-16/04/09-

Dear Journal,

Happy birthday to me. Man, high school is flying by. I have yet to make plans for what comes next. I should probably get on that.

-16/07/03-

Dear Journal,

I came with my mom today to see my dad off at the airport. Actually seeing him leave made me miss him a lot. I now see what the big deal is with my mom. I still don't know why she won't make friends. Is she like me? Or better yet, am I like her? Shit

-17/06/25-

In all my mind that my eyes can't hide is who I am when I'm awake, but something bigger is happening. I can feel it. Maybe it hasn't happened yet. Maybe it already has, or it's in the middle of happening... I don't know. I had a weird dream, that's all.

-17/06/28-

I've run away from home. My dad died in a plane crash. I made love to V at a graduation house party. I have no idea what just happened to my life. It was too much, I had to run. I have been homeless for two nights and three days. I have been travelling northwest, for no particular reason. I've been rationing the hundred dollars I got for graduation, but I don't know how many more days I can do this. I will try to get a job in the next town I find. I hope I can.

-17/08/01-

Dear Journal,
Right now I am watching the summer sun set. I feel amazing, alive. I'm filled with a visceral sense of awe, and everything is beautiful. The only things I have to my name are my clothes, my late father's jacket, my iPod and my notebook. I haven't heard any voices since I left Burlington so maybe it's better I left. I'm sleeping at a new friend of mine's place. We're co-workers together at a warehouse. He's letting me stay with him for the time being because I remind him of his little brother a bit. His brother died from a drug overdose. I'll stay for another month or two to roll up the dough, then I'll be off to the next place.

-17/12/25-

Dear Journal,

Merry Christmas! Before I write about where I am, I want to take a look back at where I was. Thinking back to what kind of a person I used to be is very strange. Like looking into a mirror and seeing someone else. I have grown so much since high school, and continue to as life goes on. I am currently living in a dodge grand caravan thanks to a good friend I made along my travels. This friend made me a fake licence and passport, making my job opportunities skyrocket. I tried ketamine for the first time with him and somehow talked my way into getting them for free. The K was fun, (except for the fact that the older woman's voice came back asking for me to heed her.) so I decided I have to stay sober, conserve my money, and keep my wits about me. My adult life has only just begun.

-18/02/12-

It's fucking cold. Just thought I'd write that in here. And I'm still being tormented by the woman's voice. She keeps whispering in my head and I can't fucking take it!

-18/09/22-

Hey, dear diary, so I'm in-between jobs at the moment. I don't have the van anymore, and I'm really fucking hungry. I was so hungry today that I heard the woman's voice call my name. My real name, Nathan. Not fucking Amon Lurani. I don't want to steal, but I don't want to die. I need a job.

-19/04/09-

Dear Journal,

Update: I'm not dead. I had hard times to say the least, but

I pulled through. Today is my birthday. I'm twenty years old now. Wow. To put it down in paper like that makes it feel a hell of a lot more real. It's been a time living this life, and there's so much more to go… Every now and again, V passes my mind. This is the life she wanted. Why didn't we go together? Fuck. That's the one thing above the rest that I'll regret for the rest of my life. I love you V.

-19/10/13-

Dear Journal,

It's getting chilly again. I just signed for an apartment in Edmonton, Alberta. Making me a long way from home. The job I got right now pays enough for me to afford rent, but I'm going to need something better if I don't want my savings to sink. It took me a long time to save the money I have now.

-19/12/25-

Dear Journal,

Merry Christmas again! I took the luxury of buying myself a two-thousand-nine Nissan Altima. It runs good with only a hundred thousand kilometres on it. For a car as old as it is, I got it in great condition for an amazing price. I'm hoping that now with a car I can find better employment. There's a place on the edge of the city called Arborlist which I might try. I've never cut down trees before. But then again, I never made tires before, or patios and decks, shingled roofs or hauled rock. But now I can say that I have. So times change, and I'll pick it up.

-20/02/14-

Hey, so first off I am a little surprised I am still writing in this thing. Am I doing it for a particular reason? Who knows? Anyway, life so far has been great. I've been making it by relatively well as far as money goes. And today I went grocery shopping and met a woman named Amy. We talked and shopped. Shopped and talked. Amy is a single mother of a four-year-old named Mason. She's only a year older than me. We hit it off so well that she gave me her number. I'm going to call her; I just don't know when. Should I do it today? Like right now? Because it's Valentine's Day and all? Ehhh, I'll hold off.

-20/03/01-

Amy is officially the first woman I have ever dated. She and I went on our second date tonight. Things were going great. We went bowling, then we went to the movies. Afterwards she asked if I wanted to come back to her house, to meet Mason. I agreed, but was feverish about it. I met Amy's mom, then Mason. He had spiked-up blonde hair, as blonde as his mom's. Amy's mom took Mason to his bed, and when we were alone, she made out with me. Fast and rough, like she was waiting the whole night for us to be by ourselves or something. In retrospect I don't know why I did it, but I stopped her. I asked if she wanted to talk about Mason's father. She didn't, but for my sake she told me. He was football player in high school. They were in love. He impregnated her, then a week later, had his neck snapped in a game. She told me she didn't want anything to change between us now that she told me that. I told her it wouldn't, but it did. I told her I'd call her tomorrow, but I don't know if I can. Loss of father who didn't even know he was a father. Now I'm supposed to take his place? I can't be a father. I'm still growing up. Amy is nice, but I can't see her again.

-20/03/10-

I feel like fucking shit about the Amy situation. But

that's not why I'm writing, just wanted to get that out there. I'm writing to let you know that tomorrow I start work at Arborlist. I start in the middle of the week, which I find a little weird, but better sooner than later.

-21/04/19-

Spring again, a bitter-sweet promise, for better things that never come. Today is my "birthday", making this the year: twenty-twenty-one. I haven't written in this thing in a long time, but something's happened. After two years of not hearing any voices I had a dream again like the one from graduation, where I woke up wondering if what I saw was actually real... I can still hear the woman's voice. She said something like: Save the man in flight, accept the killer's kiss... and, you will begin, or something along those lines. I don't know why it came back. I'm going to try harder to remember everything next time it happens and write it down. I have a strong feeling it means something. I mean it has to, I just don't know what. I don't know what to make of it, except that maybe I'm fucking insane.

-21/04/28-

Dear Journal,

Times have very much changed. V is again in my life and I am willing to do anything to keep her close. My occupation was the first sacrifice. The next was my apartment, and my sense of security. Last Saturday her and I ate shrooms for the first time. My dreams have been strange since late June of my graduation, and now I might have an idea as of why. The older woman is no woman, but a creature. I still have no idea about my ghost sister, but like all things I believe that time will tell. No longer should I think of my dreams as strange. They may just verge on prophetic. If they truly somehow are, then a terrible fate lies on this world... and what? Am I really supposed to stop it? How? I won't give up on my sanity so easily. On that I remain heavily sceptical.

On another note I also had dream last night. I was riding down a highway alone and there was something in the sky. I don't know what, but now not to jump to conclusions, but something also happened last night right before I passed out. I think I might actually have moved something... without touching it. Actually I'm certain I did.

Precognition. Telekinetic, fucking, manipulation... With no time I've actually had to ponder the possible theories that could explain everything that's been happening to me, all that I can think of now is that it has something to do with the shrooms? But there's more to it than that. People don't just gain super powers from doing drugs. The back of my head is still tingling a little. I don't know if that has to do with the sweats I've been having or not, but- oh yeah! The word- which I'll now use in extreme caution: DAWN REDWOOD, allows me to perceive everything at a higher rate. Like a Kung Fu master or something. I'll try to watch that... but seriously. To transcend the physical bounds of my body is... super, powers. I mean just to think of the things I could potentially do! I could use these powers, tread paths of glory for others to follow in.

-21/04/30-

Dear Journal,

I've thought of a name for my ability. It will be called: Telekinetic Vibrational Manipulation; the acronym for which is T.V.M. My party of nomad punks continue to travel east and to the south, though in my heart I ache to go northwest and I don't know why. However, my heart can ache all it likes because no matter how much I want anything else, V will come first, even before myself. A few weeks ago word came from my old region saying Skull the flied murderer and attempter rapist is now back. I've never met the man but just through stories I know that he may be the first man I truly hate. No one has talked about it since Sal brought it up but I know we are all thinking about it. I'm additionally thinking about my powers that I use in secret, and my dreams that scream urgency at me. The People's Deviants are my family now, and I'm in love. How could I possibly give up this freedom?

-21/06/02-

And how was I supposed to feel? That's the first thing that popped into my head after writing the date. What would I even do? Go to the nearest government building and say, excuse me but I have the ability to hover logs, may I be of assistance to you on the matter of the meteorites? It's stupid. Stupid and impossible. I can't even muster the courage to tell the gang. Somehow in a way I miss the old days of my adult life. Back then I would have written this:

Dear the coming summer, please bring me peace. Shine on me joy. Something of my childhood, when everything was so big, and new, and endless. I can remember the feeling, but I can't FEEL it anymore. Winters have made me bitter and lame; a cruel indignation. A four-year death season, now coming to a close. Come the summer, and I will be a blossoming tulip to the nuance of festivities. I wait for the day now, when it all comes back to me.

-//-

The synapses in my mind have just now finally given me a memory of my childhood of bliss. I remember poking my head out of a pile of leaves to surprise my parents in our front lawn. I must have been four. The sun has a strange way of poking itself out from the horizon to surprise us all every morning. It always seems to go slow when you focus on it but look away and in the blink of an eye everything around you is as bright as its maker. The planet slings around the star with a dizzying spin and we all go in and out of focus. What really matters in the end? My attention is with V but it keeps being pulled at to look towards the future. This gang of brothers will fall apart, the stars will rain fire, and I will hold V's hand. How selfish of me. I wish I could just go back, knowing everything I know now and take my time; but this is life, and you can never go back.

\*

# Fun Facts

\*\*

1.) The novel was originally a film script, but had been rewritten after many people in the author's life suggested so.

2.) The novel was written in the autumn of 2014, but takes place in the spring of 2017.

3.) At the beginning of the first chapter, the starry night sky is described as having no moon. The actual lunar calendar says that on the night of June 24th, 2017, there will be no moon in the night sky.

4.) The Cathedral Basilica of Christ the King is the same Cathedral the author graduated in.

5.) The iPhone 7-pro existing in the spring of 2017 was an educated guess, time will tell for that one.

6.) In the 5th chapter when Nathan drives from Edmonton to Burlington, it only takes him 29 hours, when it would really have taken him 39 hours.

7.) The entire raw plot of True Volition was done by

the time Nathan became a member of the bike gang in the original script.

8.) In the sixth chapter when Nathan is riding up highway 830 in the early morning of April 28, 2021, the lunar calendar does schedule an almost full moon.

9.) In Nathan's journal when he writes, 'Somehow in a way I miss the old days of my adult life. Back then I would have written this,' it is a nod to the fact that the first draft when the poem was written was done so when the author was 21. He edited the novel two years later and added the beginning to the journal entry.

10.) There is no run-down part of Toronto that houses a parking garage with the address 2001, that the author knows of.

11.) The lunar calendar gives June 25th, 2021 a full moon.

12.) Albert Einstein, Steven Hawking and many more scientists are certain that time travel to the past is impossible, due to such things as the grandfather paradox. Astral travel to other universes however, may be theoretically plausible. Other universes, that may be taking place seconds, or even years in the past...